T0022737

Dedalus European Classics
General Editor: Timothy Lane

MARIANNA SIRCA

Grazia Deledda

MARIANNA SIRCA

translated and with an introduction
by
Graham Anderson

Dedalus

Supported using public funding by
**ARTS COUNCIL
ENGLAND**

Published in the UK by Dedalus Limited
24-26, St Judith's Lane, Sawtry, Cambs, PE28 5XE
info@dedalusbooks.com
www.dedalusbooks.com

ISBN printed book 978 1 915568 34 2
ISBN ebook 978 1 915568 40 3

Dedalus is distributed in the USA & Canada by SCB Distributors
15608 South New Century Drive, Gardena, CA 90248
info@scbdistributors.com   www.scbdistributors.com

Dedalus is distributed in Australia by Peribo Pty Ltd
58, Beaumont Road, Mount Kuring-gai, N.S.W. 2080
info@peribo.com.au   www.peribo.com.au

First published by Dedalus in 2023
Marianna Sirca translation copyright © Graham Anderson 2023

The right of Graham Anderson to be identified as the editor & translator of this work has been asserted by him in accordance with the Copyright, Designs and Patents Act, 1988.

Printed and bound in the UK by Clays Elcograf S.p.A.
Typeset by Marie Lane

A C.I.P. listing for this book is available on request.

THE AUTHOR

GRAZIA DELEDDA

Grazia Deledda was born in 1871 in Nuoro, Sardinia. The street where she was born has been renamed after her, via Grazia Deledda. She finished her formal education at age eleven. She published her first short story when she was sixteen and her first novel, *Stella D'Oriente* in 1890 in a Sardinian newspaper when she was nineteen. She left Nuoro for the first time in 1899 and settled in Cagliari, the principal city of Sardinia where she met the civil servant Palmiro Madesani whom she married in 1900. They then moved to Rome.

Grazia Deledda wrote her best work between 1903-1920 and established an international reputation as a novelist. Nearly all of her work in this period was set in Sardinia. She published *Elias Portolu* in 1903, *La Madre* in 1920 and won the Nobel Prize for Literature in 1926. She died in 1936 and was buried in the church of Madonna della Solitudine in Nuoro, near to where she was born.

THE TRANSLATOR

GRAHAM ANDERSON

Graham Anderson was born in London. After reading French and Italian at Cambridge, he worked on the book pages of *City Limits* and reviewed fiction for *The Independent* and *The Sunday Telegraph*. As a translator, he has developed versions of French plays, both classic and contemporary, for the NT and the Gate Theatre, with performances both here and in the USA. Publications include *The Figaro Plays* by Beaumarchais and *A Flea in her Ear* by Feydeau.

His translations for Dedalus include *Sappho* by Alphonse Daudet, *Chasing the Dream* and *A Woman's Affair* by Liane de Pougy, *This was the Man (Lui)* by Louise Colet and *This Woman, This Man (Elle et Lui)* by George Sand. He has also translated Grazia Deledda's short story collections *The Queen of Darkness* and *The Christmas Present*.

His own short fiction has won or been shortlisted for three literary prizes. He is married and lives in Oxfordshire.

INTRODUCTION

D. H. Lawrence and his wife Frieda are on a bus, exploring the hinterland of Sardinia. It is a February afternoon in 1921.

'Turning sharp to the right we ran in silence over the moorland-seeming slopes, and saw the town beyond, a little below, at the end of a long declivity, with sudden mountains rising around it. There it lay, as if at the end of the world, mountains rising sombre behind... we slip into the cold high street of Nuoro. I am thinking that this is the home of Grazia Deledda, the novelist, and I see a barber's shop. Deledda. And thank heaven we are at the end of the journey. It is past four o'clock.'

They check in at an inn, then set off on foot to see the town.

'We came to the end of the street, where there is a wide, desolate sort of gap... there was a café in this sort of piazza — not a piazza at all, a formless gap... but I knew it would be hopeless to ask for anything but cold drinks or black coffee: which we did not want. So we continued forward, up the slope of the village street. These towns soon come to an end. Already we were wandering into the open... we came to the end of the houses and looked over the road-wall at the hollow, deep, interesting valley below. Away on the other side rose a blue mountain, a steep but stumpy cone. High land reared up, dusky and dark-blue, all around. Somewhere far off the sun was setting with a bit of crimson. It was a wild, unusual landscape, of unusual shape. The hills seemed so untouched, dark-blue, virgin-wild, the hollow cradle of the valley was cultivated like a tapestry away below. And there seemed so little outlying life: nothing. No castles even. In Italy and Sicily castles perching everywhere. In Sardinia none — the remote, ungrappled hills rising darkly, standing outside of life.'

At the time of the Lawrences' visit, Grazia Deledda, the novelist, was living in Rome. She had married and left her native island in 1900. But she had taken with her nearly thirty years of life among the remote, ungrappled hills, and the evocation of this lonely place, its inhabitants' way of life, their ancient customs and close-knit families, had become the subject of her prolific output. In all, she wrote over thirty novels, two hundred and fifty short stories and two plays. It was an astonishing transformation for a young woman no one had heard of, from a small town that very few had heard of.

She was born in Nuoro in September 1871, the fifth of seven children, to a fairly prosperous family, although her mother spoke no Italian, only the island language, Sard. Deledda herself had a brief elementary schooling lasting just five years, before receiving lessons at home from an Italian tutor. But she had immediately been seized with a passion for reading, and the tutor's books, along with those from the library of her uncle, a priest, formed the basis of her ongoing education and the inspiration behind her desire to emulate the authors she admired. A story published soon after her move to Rome, *The Queen of Darkness* (1902), tells the tale of a young woman's mysterious spiritual sickness, a gradual dissolution of the soul which is only remedied when the young woman, in a flash of understanding, realises that her real purpose in life, her calling, is to become a writer and to describe through her art the people and surroundings which have shaped her identity.

Already, as a teenage girl, Deledda had begun to write poems and short stories of her own. She found outlets for their publication in a number of Sardinian magazines and periodicals, for she was a bold and persistent pursuer of local and regional editors. She even wrote to the Rome-based fashion magazine *L'ultima moda*, who published some of her early works in the late 1880s. Her first novel, *Stella d'Oriente*, a romance, appeared in 1890; her second, *Fior di Sardegna*, the following year. *Racconti sardi* and *Tradizioni popolari di Nuoro in Sardegna*, both in 1894, were early examples of her life-long interest in collecting and preserving the folk tales and customs of her island. It was in 1896 that the distinguished writer and critic Luigi Campuana wrote a long and detailed appreciation of her novel *La via del male* (*The Way of Evil*) and enabled Deledda to consider herself ready for a wider stage. Nuorese life may have been the subject of her fictions, but the constraints of its reality were becoming burdensome. It was not thought fitting that a young woman, at that period and in that society, should wish to take up a literary career at all, still less use her fellow citizens and the poor and struggling rural peasants as her material.

Needing to find a way out, she was introduced, on a visit to Cagliari in 1899, to a handsome and kindly member of the island's civil service, Palmiro Madesani, and in a matter of months they were married. Madesani's transfer to the Finance Ministry in Rome, arranged in part through Deledda's powers of persuasion, enabled the couple to make the move in March 1900. In December of that year, their first son, Sardus, was born; and in 1904 their second, Francesco. The new environment swiftly brought Deledda wider recognition. Her 1900 novel, *Elias Portolu* — and particularly its French translation in the prestigious Paris journal *La revue des deux mondes* in 1903 — became her first true success. Its subject, the inappropriate relationship that forms between Elias, an ex-convict, and his brother's fiancée, the muddled and indecisive debate in Elias' mind, his eventual retreat into the priesthood, his mixed feeling after the deaths of the other two, the awareness of rules observed but lives left unfulfilled — all these were to become significant themes in Deledda's later works.

She published a new book almost every year. Notable novels included *Cenere* (*Ashes*, 1904), *L'ombra del passato* (*The Shadow of the Past*, 1907), *L'edera* (*The Ivy*, 1908) and *Canne al vento* (*Reeds in the Wind*, 1913). *Marianna Sirca* came out in 1915, at what might be considered the mid-point of her mature career. *La madre* (*The Mother*, 1920) has come to be regarded as one of her most intense and representative pieces, the story of a young priest, his poor but ambitious mother, and the young woman with whom he falls in love.

Grazia Deledda was now 49, and although she could not have known it, the 35-year-old DH Lawrence was well aware of her presence on the literary scene, as witnessed in the excerpt above from his travel book *Sea and Sardinia* (US, 1921; UK, 1923). Further works continued to pour from her pen: three in 1921 alone, one in 1922, two more in 1923, notably *Silvio Pellico. La fuga in Egitto* (*The Flight Into Egypt*, 1925) was the most recent novel she had published when the news came that the committee in Stockholm had awarded her the 1926 Nobel Prize in Literature. She collected it at a ceremony in Sweden the following year, managing only the briefest of speeches. Although a warm and relaxed woman in familiar company, her basically reserved nature made public appearances a trial. Her ambition was certainly fierce, but she was wary of the unknown and preferred to live quietly, away from the spotlight.

Episodes of ill health had begun to occur at about this time. Breast cancer was eventually diagnosed and a successful operation performed. She continued to write, industrious and disciplined. Many of her later books were lighter and more optimistic in tone: the collection of stories, fables and girlhood reminiscences of *Il dono di natale* (*The Christmas Present*, 1930), the novels *Il paese del vento* (*The Land of the Wind*, 1931) and *Sole d'estate* (*Summer Sun*, 1933) being examples. Her health, however deteriorated in the following years, and she died, in Rome, in August 1936, a few weeks short of her 65th birthday.

Marianna Sirca, her novel of 1915, is both typical and unusual. Its setting, once again, is Nuoro and the surrounding sheep pastures and cork-oak forests. Poverty and relative affluence live side by side. Born in a humble situation, Marianna is placed when still a child in the household of her uncle, a priest and owner of a comfortable house in the town. Her father, Berte Sirca, an efficient farmer but in other respects a weak man, hopes his only daughter will enjoy a better life than he can provide for her on their *tanca* up in the hills. And indeed, on the priestly uncle's death, Marianna inherits everything, the farm holdings as well as the house. But she has become *la padrona* at a cost. Her youth has been lost, spent effectively in service to the uncle. The elderly servant Fidela is her only companion in the Nuoro house. Her older cousin Sebastiano, a sometimes mocking, sometimes wistful admirer, makes her uncomfortable. She is already thirty, yet feels she has never truly lived.

The unexpected reappearance of a young man who was once a servant alongside her in the priest's house completely upsets her uneventful life of obedience to the wishes of others. This man, after many failed attempts to get on in life, has run away to become a bandit. It may be hard to imagine that outlaws still existed at the turn of the twentieth century, but the remoteness of Sardinia from the mainland and its modern ways, the long tradition of rugged self-survival, of family feuds settled by violence, of lives — criminal or merely escapist — being lived outside the community, still persisted. Simone Solo, as it turns out, is a sadly ineffectual bandit. He commits small robberies but is insufficiently ruthless to spill Christian blood. Inside him though, is a burning rage at the injustices of life. He despises the poverty into which his family, a sick father, a careworn mother and five sisters, has fallen. The disparity between his lot and Marianna's is simultaneously a source of attraction and resentment.

When Marianna and Simone meet again after many years,

a spark is ignited. Marianna has never loved, never been courted, never been allowed to make her own choices. Simone is driven by a dangerous mixture of emotional neediness and powerful self-regard. In bringing such opposite characters together, Deledda is not simply writing a romance between the repressed spinster and the dashing young outlaw. She is examining the clash between two ways of life — both of them unsatisfactory — and the constraints forced on all levels of Nuorese society by the haphazard distribution of wealth and the strict social conventions of the time. The damaged individuals who emerge from this society have little but pride and a sense of their personal dignity to keep them in balance. It is this pride, which both parties have in their different ways, which turns their brave hopes into disaster.

The idea for this novel allows Deledda to explore her native district in its three distinctive topographical settings: the rugged hills where the bandits live; the forests and farmsteads where the great majority earn their living; and the brooding and enclosed life of the town itself. It is all just as Lawrence sensed it to be in 1921, half a dozen years after *Marianna Sirca* was published. Motor buses and metalled roads may have come to inland Sardinia, as they had not yet done in Deledda's early years; but old costumes were still seen on the streets, old customs still observed in the houses of the wealthy and the hovels of the poor. And in the hills, before the modern age of kidnap and ransom, bandits still lived, singly or in gangs, with a price on their heads.

Martha King's biography *Grazia Deledda, A Legendary Life*, and her English translations of *Elias Portolu* and an autobiographical novel, *Cosima*, published the year after Deledda's death, are highly recommended to interested readers. D. H. Lawrence's *Sea and Sardinia* can be found with a little internet research.

Meanwhile the unique voice of the Nobel Prize winning Grazia Deledda can be sampled in Dedalus Books' 2021 re-issue of *La madre*, translated by M. G. Steegman. And along with the present novel, Dedalus also publishes Deledda's early and later short story collections *The Queen of Darkness* (*La regina delle tenebre*, 1902) and *The Christmas Present* (*Il dono di natale*, 1930).

I

After the death of her uncle, Marianna Sirca had gone to spend
a few days in a little farmhouse she owned in the Sierra above
Nuoro, in the midst of the cork oak forest. The uncle, a priest
and a wealthy man, had died recently, leaving his estate to her.

It was June. Her uncle had lain paralysed for two long
years. Worn out by nursing him at his bedside all that time,
Marianna was so pale, so weak, so dazed, it seemed she had just
emerged from prison. And she would not have moved on her
own account, nor taken any notice of the doctor's advice to get
away and breathe some purer air, if her father, who was a sheep
farmer and had always been a sort of servant to his priestly
brother, had not expressly come down from the mountains to
collect her, respectfully imploring her: 'Marianna, listen to the
people who love you. Do as they say.'

The housekeeper at Nuoro, a coarse, energetic woman

from the wilds of Barbagia who had been with the priest for years and had seen Marianna grow up, assembled her belongings, cramming them roughly into the knapsack as if they belonged to a humble shepherd, and she too repeated: 'Marianna, listen to the people who love you: do as they say.'

And Marianna had obeyed. She had always obeyed, ever since she had been placed in her uncle's house to spread around the melancholy priest the light and joy of her young girlhood. She was to be his little caged bird, in exchange for a possible inheritance.

So she climbed up silently behind her father on his horse and gripped his belt, only nodding her head in reply to the zealous servant who was arranging her skirts around her legs and advising her not to catch cold in the night air.

'And don't tire her out, Berte Sirca!'

The latter put a finger to his lips and dug his heels into the horse's flanks. He too was a man of few words, and in any case, with Marianna, they had little to say to each other.

As they travelled, he merely pointed out a field here and there, naming its owner. She knew these places anyway, because every year in spring, except for the last few when the priest had been ill, she used to go with him and various other relations to spend whole days on the *tanca*, the enclosed pastures where he kept his flocks of sheep and herds of cattle; and where a little farmhouse had replaced the usual primitive cabin of the Sardinian shepherds.

From the first day up there in the hills she felt better. The *tanca* occupied a high position on the border of the Nuoro and Orune districts. The forest trees were in blossom and an infinite serenity seemed to stretch across the whole land.

By the third day Marianna already seemed a different person. The thin and slightly stooping figure had straightened. The alabaster-pale face beneath the sweeping tresses of glossy black hair had taken on a dull amber colouring and her large and placid brown eyes reflected like a fawn's the greenish light of the woods.

As evening fell on the third day, she was sitting outside the farmhouse. A small building of undressed stone, it had a shelter for the animals, a kitchen and a bedroom. Before her she could see a broad grassy clearing with an ancient cork oak in the middle, the dogs tethered to its trunk. And beyond it the green of the meadows which stretched as far as the forest and lost themselves in the already darkening shadows of the thickets of scrub and outcrops of rock. Meanwhile, to her right, through a line of trees, the ridge of mountains stood out, still blue, against the reddening sky of dusk.

She was alone except for the dogs, who rose every now and then to stare out across the landscape and soon came back to crouch in the dust. But she was expecting her father and the shepherd to return soon, and also awaiting the arrival of a relation who had promised her a visit.

She was alone and at peace. She wanted for nothing. Around her she had her extensive inheritance, looked after by the reliable hand of the simple soul, her father. And down in Nuoro her house too was looked after, by the faithful servant who did not sleep at night, for ever on watch against thieves.

She wanted for nothing. And yet, a private and introspective woman, what she saw when she looked inward, with full self-knowledge, was a kind of twilight. It may have been serene, yes, but with a quality of dusk nevertheless: red and grey, grey and red, and as solitary as the dusk filling the sheep pen.

It seemed to her that she was old. She could see herself as a child in this very same place, the first time they had brought her up here and someone had whispered in her ear: if you're a good girl, all this will be yours. And she had gazed all around, with neither wonder nor desire in her placid eyes, just saying yes. And exploring in this direction and that, never wandering too far in case she got lost, she had found a den, a rock scooped out like a cradle, and squeezed herself into it, very pleased to be alone, mistress of all but hidden from everything. And she felt like the stone inside the fruit, the little bird inside the egg. In such a fashion, nestled away, pleased that the shepherds did not catch at her petticoat as she passed, saying, with a wink, 'why not share your little den with me, Marianna?' she had even fallen asleep there.

And now she was waking up, after so many years. Thirty of them already, and still she scarcely knew anything of love. They had brought her up seemingly as a girl from a noble family, destined for a rich marriage. In reality, her life had been that of a serving girl, subservient not only to her masters but to the servants of higher rank than herself.

But here was her father coming back. And her thoughts retreated into their most secret hiding place. No one in the world must know them, not so much out of pride as because in her mind, as in her house, she liked everything to be in order, cleaned, tidied away, belonging to herself alone.

In any event her father, even if he felt for her an unspoken admiration and a faithful servant's attachment, was not a man capable of understanding her. Here he was, coming nearer, short, stooping, hands clasped together, his large bald head seemingly weighed down over his chest by the long grey curling beard. He resembled a holy brother in shepherd's clothes, a gentle hermit with his great, still innocent, chestnut brown eyes.

'What's this, are you praying?' he said, walking past her. 'Come on, cheer up, we're celebrating tonight. They're coming up.'

'Who, who?' she said, looking round.

'Sebastiano and another man. I'm lighting the fire now. If Sebastiano asks you how much they've offered you for the cork,' he added, turning back, 'tell him a thousand *scudi*. Hush! Listen to the people who love you.'

Marianna was ready to obey even this innocent vanity of his, which doubled the value of her harvest. All the more so since her relative, Sebastiano, was coming on behalf of certain dealers from Ozieri who wanted to acquire the cork from her oak woods. And without getting up, she narrowed her eyes, thinking of her second cousin, a man neither young nor old, neither rich nor poor, a widower and alone; and the only one, amongst so many needy relations bearing her a grudge over her uncle's inheritance, to show her a little disinterested affection.

At times, she had suspected that Sebastiano loved her more deeply, but she rejected with distaste the idea of ending up the wife of a relative, a widower who was no longer young. And now here he came as well: he was on horseback; he was wearing the short cape of widowed men, and the black velvet of his coat caused the yellowish pallor of his face to stand out even from a distance, a narrow face ringed by a sparse little beard, dark and pointed. The large and gleaming dark eyes which illuminated his whole sad face immediately sought out

Marianna; and almost before he had dismounted in front of her she had risen silently to her feet. He put an arm round her shoulders, looking her up and down, a little smaller than she was, familiar but somehow sly as well. She pushed him away, however, intent only on a tall and handsome young man advancing towards her with a smile. She thought she didn't know him, yet also felt that she did. She seemed to have seen that mouth before, the teeth gleaming between fresh lips shaded by a downy moustache, and in that tanned face the long narrow eyes which appeared dark blue against the pale azure of the whites.

Coming up to her, he stopped, stood stiff, a soldier at attention. She blushed, but suddenly smiled and stretched out her hand.

'Simone Sole!'

He nodded, taking her hand without squeezing it. Yes, it was him, Simone Sole, the bandit.

Some years before, as a boy, Simone had been a servant in her house. She knew the family too: poor but distinguished, of good stock, the father and mother both delicate, the sisters beautiful, proud young women who left their house only to go to church and who knelt in the shadows, where she too would usually be, beneath the altar of the sacrament. For the rest of the time they lived withdrawn in their little house under the hill of Santu Nofre, silent and grieving as if their brother were dead.

'Simone,' she repeated in a calm voice, having lowered her eyes then raised them placidly again to face him. 'Well then?'

'Well then, we're here!'

And he continued to smile at her, his handsome teeth pressed together like a child trying to hold back a burst of laughter. He seemed pleased to have given her a surprise, but more than anything he was pleased at her welcome.

'So, Marianna, have you come to roam the hills like a bandit as well?'

They both laughed, a little, as if sharing the joke. Quickly, however, Marianna saw the other's eyes seek hers in a glance that disturbed her. And as he drew close enough to brush against her knees, she took a step back, aloof.

Meanwhile the father had appeared in the kitchen doorway, wiping his blood-stained hand on his trousers, and gesturing with a jerk of the head for the guests to step forward, to enter the house. They went in, and despite the heat, sat down round the hearth.

Simone looked about him, greeting the things he recognised so well: the smoke-blackened walls, the low bed, the mats on which he had slept his long adolescent slumbers, the simple benches, the cork-wood vessels, the skins and the stones and all the other household objects which smelled of cheese and hide and gave the rough room the feeling of the kind of tent inhabited by shepherds in the bible. Through the open doorway, opposite the small window with its background view of the green forest, could be glimpsed the little adjoining room, which also had a door opening on to the clearing. The impression of cleanliness, with Marianna's little white bed, the table, a picture and a little mirror on the wall, made a marked contrast with the kitchen.

She closed the communicating door and sat at Sebastiano's shoulder, because she became aware that he was following her with a roguish eye, not at all disconcerted, as she went about her business. But he swivelled sideways and continued to watch her.

'Marianna!' said Simone. 'I feel I'm dreaming, seeing you again.'

'It feels the same to me, Simone!'

'I'd wanted to visit you for such a long time! But I didn't know if you'd welcome it…'

Marianna waved a hand to signal he should stop, that remarks along such lines were needless. And he blushed, out of pride at her faith in him.

'How is it you're in these parts? It's a good while since anyone's seen you,' the father said; while Sebastiano, taking the edge of Marianna's apron, pulled it a little towards him, making gestures with his head for her to lean over, that he had something to tell her in secret. She remained bolt upright. It seemed to her that Simone was in his turn observing her and she wished to appear to him in full possession of her new status as a serious woman, a rich property owner. Simone was indeed looking at her, even while answering the questions of the man who had once been his companion in service more than his master.

'Yes, it was nearly a year ago I last came this way, zio Berte. It's already been five years since I last saw your Marianna. So the Canon is dead? What a strange man he was! Marianna, do you remember how he used to add years to his real age? Ten, he added. Maybe he thought life sounded too short otherwise, for a man in good health as he was. And he once got furious because his servant, Fidela (is she still alive, Lord help us?) went to church and had someone look up his real age in the records.'

'That's right, yes, and maybe it was so he could believe he was living longer,' added Sebastiano. 'And then in his case, those years were spent well, and he was right to add a few on.'

'And those who take years off, isn't that worse. Women? And certain men as well? Look at our Cristoru over there: he's always twenty-two!'

Everyone laughed, looking outside towards the vast and swarthy figure of the servant who was approaching, his body moving stiffly, all of a piece, as if he was made of wood. Coming up to the doorway he stopped, without showing any surprise at the presence of Simone, who had been his companion in service. And for all that the two guests called to him, asking after his health, the animals, the shepherds on the neighbouring *tanca*, he made no move to step over the threshold.

He wanted Marianna, and Marianna had to go outside into the clearing to discuss dinner arrangements with him.

'Your father sent me to slaughter a sheep. Tell me what I'm to cook, and if I'm to prepare a blood pudding as well. I warn you though, I haven't any mint; I've only got two bay leaves, here they are.'

He held them up for her to see between his blood-stained fingers, and she went off to fetch salt as well, cheese and a small piece of the ground-barley bread. These things were all mixed together and stuffed inside the sheep's heart, washed and cleaned like a velvety pouch; and the heart was then sewn up with a bamboo needle and put to cook under a heap of hot ashes.

Meanwhile the men were discussing the price of cork,

and the father was saying, looking at the ground because he didn't know how to lie, that the merchants from Ozieri had offered a thousand *scudi*. But Sebastiano laughed, his dark eyes gleaming in his sallow face, and looked at Marianna with a wink.

'Zio Berte, you know how to talk up your wares all right!'

'They're not mine because they're my daughter's!'

'They're yours because they're mine,' Marianna retorted, and the father was very happy because he felt Sebastiano was making fun of him.

Marianna, during all this, was bent over the hearth, helping the servant prepare the dinner. She had pushed back the folds of her black scarf, so that they lay on the top of her head, leaving her white neck and rosy throat exposed. In the reflections from the fire, the gold buttons of her blouse, drawn together by a green ribbon, gleamed pinkly like two half-ripe strawberries, and every now and then she glanced at them as if afraid they might come loose, but in reality because she was aware of Simone's gaze fixed on her. She felt obscurely troubled. She almost felt timid about turning to face him, yet he had been her inferior in service. He seemed to her like a man returned from foreign lands, where he had grown up, where he had become a man and had learnt all the bad things and also the good things in life, like the emigrants who returned from the Americas. Precisely because of this, however, she also felt pleasure in being watched by him: in the end, it was the look of a man who saw in her only the woman, without thinking about her money.

When the dinner was ready, she sat among the men round the well-furnished table set on the ground before the open door. The table was a slab of cork-wood, a whole slice cut from a tree, split and planed smooth; and the trays and bowls were of cork-wood too and the cups were of horn, fashioned by the shepherds. The impassive giant of a servant acted as carver, breaking the bones away from the roast with his powerful fingers. When he had finished dividing the meat into portions, he pushed the trencher in front of Marianna, saying in his heavy voice: 'Put the salt on.'

And she took salt between her fingers with the same delicacy with which she had mixed the bay leaves with the blood, sprinkled it gravely, head bowed, over the fragrant roast.

They ate in silence. The red moon rose like a peaceful fire between the oaks at the bottom of the clearing, lighting the meadows with a blood-coloured glow. The woman, with her scarlet bodice rendered more vivid by the light of the flames from the hearth, shone amidst the black figures of the men like the moon between the tree trunks.

After the roast, the servant pulled the blood pudding from the ashes, cleaned it a little, split it in pieces and again placed the dish before Marianna.

'Put the salt on.'

It seemed as if they were accomplishing a rite, the servant standing stiffly with his square black beard like an Egyptian priest's, she pale and slender in her bodice, like a pomegranate flower.

Simone was the first to be served.

'It's not every evening you share your bread with a woman,' said zio Berte, pouring him a drink in his horn cup.

'And what a woman!' Simone promptly replied, drinking

and looking at her. And it seemed to her that the wine gleamed through the translucent vessel.

'All the same, Simone ate last night with some women, and pretty ones too, besides Marianna!' Sebastiano said, jealous.

Marianna looked up.

'That was my sisters, yes. I was at home because my mother is ill.'

A moment of silence, solemn and sad; then Marianna asked, quietly: 'How is your mother now?'

'Ah, her usual trouble, the heart. My sisters are brave on their own account, but they easily take fright on someone else's. So they sent for me, to go and see my mother. The trouble is that if I go to see her, there's a danger of something worse happening: and she knows that very well! Last night I didn't dare enter her room; but she said: "My Simone must be near, I can sense it. Bring him in." So I went in; and she put her hand on my head and begged me to get away at once. Well, that's the way of the world!' he concluded, twitching his head aside in a childish gesture Marianna had seen him make from boyhood.

'Ah!' Berte Sirca sighed as well; and Sebastiano did not persist in his jokes.

Only the servant remained stern, impassive, as if nothing concerned him except his duties. And yet it was he who dispersed the shadow that had fallen on those around, asking Simone: 'You had a partner: what happened to him? Is he inside?'

'Inside?' Simone protested, almost offended. 'As long as he's with me he'll never be taken.'

All the same he began to laugh to himself, remembering his partner.

'A little Brother, God help me! And how the fellow believes in God! He prays all the time and keeps a collection of relics hanging on a string round his neck. He only has to spot a church in the distance and he's on his knees, and the best thing, dear brethren, is that he's praying for me, not himself! And what's more, he's rich, an only son: his mother is the most well-to-do woman in Ottana, and gives him everything he wants. But he lives like a pauper, and fasts until he nearly brings on a fever.'

'God preserve me, from what you say the man's a sexton, not a bandit,' said Sebastiano, who kept looking at Marianna, sending her signs inviting her to join him in his mockery. 'And what has he done, if you please, to make him take to the forest? Did he kill a cat?'

Simone, however, would not allow them to jeer at his partner. He sent his gaze round the company, with eyes now hard as metal, and informed them gravely: 'His mother had a law suit. She had to win it and she lost. And not content with that, her adversaries went to stand under her window every night and sang obscene songs that offended her honour. She was a widow, she had no one to defend her, except Costantino, who was still a boy then, and religious, and as devoted to his mother as a daughter. And one night he got up and fired off a round from his shotgun at the men who had offended his mother. One of them fell dead. My companion wanted to hand himself over to justice; his mother advised him to run, to keep his liberty. And he ran. He did the right thing, by God!'

As he spoke, he puffed out his chest and something feline

came into his eyes, making his face more handsome: the men stared at him, nodding their heads in approval.

Only Marianna dared to reply: 'God alone has the right to take lives.'

But the servant set the conversation on a new track.

'This morning, it must have been about five, I saw a woman on horseback, down towards Funtana in Litu. She had a long man's coat, she was tall and beautiful: but that doesn't matter. She was armed, and when she saw me she spurred on her horse and disappeared. Do you think, Simone, it might have been Paska Devaddis, the woman who goes with the bandits from Orgosolo? Do you know her?'

Simone did not know her; he had never been a member of the Corraine gang, the Orgosolo bandits, and in fact took especial care to live alone, with just the young companion who had attached himself to him like a faithful dog. Nevertheless he was a friend and admirer of the Corraine band, and started to talk about them with respect. And there was then a serious discussion of the tragic fate of this family, devoured by hate: relations against relations, old men who lived on only to take revenge, women and children turned upside down in the deadly whirlwind, mothers who kept vigil at the fireside waiting in the night for the shout that announced the death of one of the sons and at dawn the cock's crow that heralded a new day of blood.

'And why does all this happen?' Marianna said in her calm voice. 'For the sake of a little wretched money! The chief reason the family is at war has been this: a few bits of money badly shared out, an inheritance unfairly divided up. Ah, but it's not money that makes people happy!'

Annoyed, Simone retorted: 'You talk like that because

you're well off in your house, and the property, it's yours, and your uncle has left you a bed of roses! But try to understand what need is; try to understand what injustice is! Marianna, a man has a right to have what belongs to him, and the real man says: what's mine is mine and woe betide anyone who lays a hand on it!'

'Nothing on this earth is ours because we are only passing through.'

Then Sebastiano caught hold of the hem of her apron again, tugging at it and shaking it, and exclaimed: 'You sound like the Canon when he was preaching, Marianna, my cousin! Well, since we're passing through, give me the cork from your oak woods for nothing! Ah, suddenly that ear's gone deaf, pretty flower of mine!'

'Even the Canon, a good soul, preached wise words but kept his keys firmly in his fist,' Simone continued. 'Yes, yes, God save me, all you rich people are like the traders at the festivals. They set their merchandise out on the ground and it looks as if they're selling it cheap, but then they sell it at a higher price than usual.'

How was she to reply, Marianna? She let it go, but she occasionally looked at Simone and every time he seemed to be waiting to catch her eye. Now he was telling them how he had recently been to consult with these same Orgosolo bandits, on business he did not explain. But that was not the point. The interesting thing was his description of the journey, up and over monte Santu Janne, down slopes, across ditches, through ravines, labyrinths, underground passages, grottos and mysterious caverns.

'Costantino followed me panting like a dog: we found

ourselves in a cave so white it seemed like marble. The vault was pierced in places and the sun came in as if filtered through a sieve. The wonderful thing is that there's an altar at the back, a real altar, with a cross, and a Christ made from the natural stone, so well carved it seemed real. Well, Costantino fell to his knees; and I did too, I'm telling the truth, I felt cold in the joints. Then above it there was a narrow passage running across, filled with rushing water which suddenly disappeared into a ravine like a stream of water poured into a glass. Corraine was waiting up there. He had come in haste and was thirsty; he bent down to drink, and God's my witness, he seemed to want to drink every drop of water in that deep glass.'

'They say he's a fine-looking man, Corraine. What's he like?' Marianna asked and Simone in turn appeared a little jealous.

'Fine-looking?... he's proud and serious. He'd be just your type, Marianna.'

'Why? It isn't good looks that make the man.'

Sebastiano began to count on his fingers.

'Wealth, no; looks, no; pride, no. What do you want then, cousin? It's like that stream: you're letting your days flow past without knowing where they'll end up.'

'And what does that matter to you? Carry on with your story, Simone: when Corraine drank...'

'When Corraine drank he wiped his mouth!'

'And was Costantino afraid?'

'Costantino was not afraid. What was he meant to be frightened of?' Simone said sharply, always ready to make fun of his partner but even more ready to defend him from other people's mockery.

'Drink up, then! Anyone would think you were more afraid of this little horn cup than of that big stone one. Drink, Simò!' zio Sirca said, good-natured and hearty.

To demonstrate that not even wine, which is one of a bandit's worst enemies, made him afraid, Simone drank; and he continued to stare at Marianna over the rim of the cup.

'Marianna, what's been happening to you all this time? Are you not thinking of taking a husband?'

'She's choosing,' Sebastiano responded on her behalf. 'She's choosing, the way you choose wild pears, looking for one that's ripe!'

She made no reply. She collected the bread, the plates, the trencher, put them in the basket and handed everything to the servant so that she could clear the table. Then she stood up and returned a few objects to their places; and since Sebastiano was making jokes, saying that zio Berte should have married the Canon's serving woman, Fidela, because it was his own bad example that was preventing Marianna from marrying, she went out into the clearing and walked up and down.

The night was warm and clear. The stars hovering over the wood seemed near enough to touch, and everything, grass, leaves, flowers, gave off a sweet scent. Marianna did not feel offended by her cousin's jesting; it only displeased her that he should talk that way in front of Simone.

Sebastiano came out to find her while her father and the servant walked across to the enclosure where the animals were penned, and said, bringing his face up close to hers: 'Don't be brusque with Simone: stay friendly with him, Marianna…'

'I don't need friends,' she replied sharply. All the same she went back inside and for a few moments found herself alone with Simone; and she noticed from his face and his whole bearing that he had somehow withdrawn into himself, with a look of tiredness and sadness.

'Drink, Simone.'

He grasped the wrist of the hand which was offering him the cup.

'Marianna, as God's my witness, you've become beautiful!' he murmured. And his eyes flashed at her, cat-like and yet sad, almost imploring. 'Marianna, do you remember when you gave me something to drink, when I used to come back from the sheep pens freezing cold?'

'I was thinking exactly of that, Simone!'

'What have you thought about me, all this time? Several times it went through my mind to come and find you; but the truth is, I was in awe of you.'

'In awe of *me*?'

'Of you, because you are proud. Even then you were proud: not with me, though, no; not then, and not even now.'

'Neither then nor now. I have no reason to be proud. So drink.'

'Marianna,' he said, taking the cup in his other hand, without letting go of her wrist. 'Yes, when they told me: Marianna is up on the Sierra, I immediately thought: I want to go and find her. Are you pleased, to see me?'

Marianna began to laugh, but at once made herself serious again, because even as he was drinking, he continued to hold her tightly by the wrist. And with her slender fingers she gripped his powerful fingers, prising them back one by one to free herself.

'Let me go,' she commanded, frowning.

He obeyed, as when he was a servant.

Unexpectedly, however, she saw him put his fingers to the ground like claws, as if he wanted to take hold of the earth, and then cock his ears to the noises coming from outside and leap to his feet, twitching all over as if to rid himself of a heavy coat. And again he seemed to her like a different person, the emancipated servant who was looking at her as equal to equal, casting off his former servitude.

But the men came back in and he said no more.

II

In the darkness of her little room, filled with the scents of the forest, Marianna was trying to get to sleep. But her mind's eye saw again the figure of Simone in the act of clawing the ground and springing up as if to assert his power over her and everything around. Yes, as if from the bare earth, he had sprung from his obscure lot as a servant to become the feared guest of his own masters. And she could see him watching her, with those soft and terrible eyes: if they had been alone, he would have fallen on her like prey.

And yet, however he acted, and although her wrist still burned from his grip, it remained clear to her that she was mistress here. She was certain that a single look from her would have brought him down to earth.

She imagined she could see him again as a boy, a young herdsman on this same property, at the beck and call of her uncle's shepherds. A tall, thin youth, skin tanned by the sun, rarely speaking, he would sit with his head lowered and slightly turned away to the right, as if preoccupied by weighty thoughts; and every now and then his head would twitch and those glowing eyes would dart all round. Every Sunday his mother would go to the masters' house to ask after him, as one might a child at school. Yes, his work and behaviour were good: he was reliable, diligent, hard-working. Towards Easter he would return home to fulfil his Easter duties, and at Christmas he accompanied the master to Midnight Mass. He did not look at women, he did not drink, he had no vices. Marianna could not remember that he had ever shown her anything less than respect. And suddenly he had absented himself from the sheep-folds one day and never come back. The family had wept for him as if for a death; it had gone on for months. Their first thought was that he must have witnessed some crime being committed, and the criminals, to protect themselves against a possibly damaging testimony, had killed him and hidden the body. Only the mother persisted in returning at intervals to Marianna to seek news, as if he were still at the farm. The mother's manner was occasionally strange: she seemed to be requesting his masters, to whom she had entrusted him while still a child, to restore her son to her.

Later, Simone had sent news, and she had shut herself away in her little house, never to step out again. Marianna, glad not to see the mother before her any more with those big eyes full of anguish and questions, had forgotten the little servant as if he really was dead. And instead, here he was now, springing up before her, rising from the tomb of his wretchedness and grabbing at everything in his reach.

'What's mine is mine and woe betide anyone who lays a hand on it!'

She remembered everything he had said, and was still trying to counter it in her thoughts. But that reply of his fell like a blow to her heart. She tossed and turned on her little bed and tried to go to sleep, smiling a little at herself. Sleep did not come. Something was getting in the way. It is him again; he is still gripping her wrist, staring at her, menacing yet imploring. Even when she dreamt, they were staring at each other as if they had known one another for years and years and one of them, him, knew the other, her, to the depths of her soul. She was speaking to him: 'I know that you like me and that you need your revenge for having been my servant once.' And he was saying in reply: 'I know that you were waiting for a man like me. Here I am. I give you all of me, the good and the bad, but I take the whole of you too, with your good and bad.'

She turned over again, annoyed, overheated. She knew very well all this was just a dream, a fantasy created in her imagination by the appearance of Simone in the solitariness of these sheep-rearing hills: a passing song like the murmuring of the forest stirred in the night by the pre-dawn winds. Perhaps Simone would never in his entire life pass by again, and yet… and yet deep down she knew already that it was not so. He would return. He had placed around her wrist a band from which it would not be easy to free herself. And once again she saw him in the act of staring at her, taking her in with a gaze as earnest as the caress of a loving hand. And looking up in the dark, she blushed on her pillow as though his face, even if only glimpsed in the insubstantiality of a dream, had brought itself close to hers and the beating of their temples had merged into a single pulse.

What if he was there, outside, and pushed at her door? 'I'm feverish,' she thought, feeling her wrist. 'Marianna, what are you doing?'

The confused murmuring of the forest answered her, calming her a little. She thought back to her house in Nuoro, warm, dark, quiet, full of precious things. She saw the servant, Fidela, who stayed awake to watch for thieves, and she smiled at herself again. 'Marianna, what are you doing?' she seemed to hear her slow, calm voice saying. 'Has a worm crawled into your brain tonight? Because a slightly tipsy man has gripped you by the wrist, does that put you in a fever? Or is it the devil tempting you? What's got into you?'

And the thought that the devil really had got into her mind and her body, in the form of Simone, brought her a sense of both anguish and shame.

'Marianna, what are you doing? Have you forgotten who you are? You are the mistress, he is the servant; you are a mature woman, he is young; you are rich and he has nothing, no home and no freedom!'

'But that's just the thing: life is more colourful when there's contrast, when there's danger, as the song says.'

'Ah, Marianna, what are you doing? He really is inside you now. This is called temptation.'

'Lord God, free me,' she murmured, pulling the sheet over her face. And she felt like a little bird hiding its head under its wing.

Simone left during the night and was not seen again for several days. Marianna did not expect him either; that much was certain. Quite the opposite: she felt she had been dreaming and had no wish even to remember the dream. At times, however, she would lift her head, thinking she heard distant footsteps, and would stand transfixed, staring into the forest.

A group of holm oaks was in flower at the far side of the meadow. The dead leaves dropped away as the new ones pushed through, and the flowers burgeoned and opened in time with the leaves. They all had the same pale gold colour, which even after the sun had gone down lent the age-old trees the splendour of full sunlight. She would linger at the little kitchen window towards evening, gazing at this brilliance shining through the dark green of the forest. She did not understand why it gave her an obscure feeling of joy to see the old oaks suddenly becoming young again and gleam with some internal light of their own. Sebastiano found her like this, at the window, pale but with shining eyes, one day when he returned to bring her the money promised for the sale of the cork. He was also in a happy mood, as he always was when he had a reason to visit her. But a shadow of jealousy came back to cloud his features when he surprised her in that attitude.

'Here,' he said, counting out the money on the narrow windowsill. 'Nobody will come and rob you while you've got such a good protector.'

Marianna felt her heart race, hidden away within her, like a bird waking up in its cage. She had understood, but wanted to know more.

'Who are you talking about? Simone? He might at least have shown his face again. Did we treat him badly, perhaps?'

'Badly? You treated him like a king, dear cousin! Only, watch yourself; don't allow him too many liberties.'

'I have never allowed anyone any liberties, and I don't

need anyone!' she retorted, indignant.

Sebastiano drew comfort from her reply, but she remained disturbed, offended by his insinuations, and deep down happy that Simone was somewhere in the vicinity.

Towards nightfall, she wandered up and down the meadow for a while, helping to bring the cows in from pasture. In the serene silence of the farmstead, the dense grass was alive with the chirring of the grasshoppers and the smallest noises were loud with echoes.

She kept thinking she heard footsteps in the distance. She walked a short way beyond the little wood of holm oaks, to a rising piece of ground from where one could look out over the track. She had never been this far, alone, at night. She wondered at the reason for such boldness. The answer came with simple directness from her heart: she hoped to meet Simone. And she was ashamed and returned to the house.

After dinner she sat outside the door of her bedroom, as she did every evening. Her father and the servant were already asleep in the kitchen, and around her all was silence, a glittering of stars, a chirring of grasshoppers. The moon sank, she sat on.

Withdrawing into herself again, it seemed to her that she had conquered her fantasies, ashamed still of her little evening stroll. And she lightly touched her cold fingers together, counting off the days that remained before she would return to her house in Nuoro. But a chill ran through her at the thought. It occurred to her that she was thinking of it as a prison.

All at once she raised her head, anxious. She heard footsteps once more, and even though judging herself mistaken, listened intently. Her heart was not deceiving her: a man was coming directly towards the house, towards her. She recognised him immediately, and held her hand to her face as if to conceal her agitation. She did not get up; she did not move.

She noticed with surprise that the dogs did not stir, even when the man passed beneath the great oak in the clearing. He walked up to the half-open kitchen door, looked inside, saw the shepherds asleep and came straight over to her.

'Good evening, Marianna. Still up?'

'Good evening, Simone. Still in these parts?'

'Still. I've been to see my mother again. She's feeling better.'

'Do you want to come in?' she asked, standing up, but he caught her by the arm and made her sit down again. And without unslinging his gun he sat next to her on the same step, breathing a little heavily as if he had been running.

Although they were so close to one another that she could sense the heat and pulse of his body, they sat without touching.

For a moment, her thoughts in confusion, she waited for him to pull her towards him, or at least take her hand; then she relaxed. They did not speak. Gradually his breathing steadied and returned to normal. After a while he stood up, adjusted the gun on his shoulder and went away, like someone who, having sat down briefly at the roadside for a rest, then resumes his journey.

He came back again on other occasions, but in the daytime, chatting with the shepherds busy at their work and hardly greeting Marianna, sitting quietly at her own work in the shade of the house.

And he seemed to her another man, a person who resembled her former young servant but stiffer, almost like a stranger. Becoming aware that he shot her furtive looks, as if still affected by the suggestion and the memory of his old state of servitude, but watching her for a gesture or a look which might invite him to be bolder, she looked him squarely in the face, firm, undaunted, yet with a tremor of sorrowful longing.

He, on the other hand, did not linger, never accepted the invitation to stay and eat and sleep with the shepherds. After that first evening the offer of hospitality appeared rather to irritate him. Only on the evening before Marianna's return to Nuoro did he alter his habit and stay late. They were out in the clearing, under the tree, and he seemed to want to say something to her at last, but was unable to find the words. Sitting on a stone, his head in his hands, he raised his eyes from time to time and she could see they were full of shadows and rapidly changing lights. He would stare out into the distance, then close in on himself once more, searching for something.

Finally he asked: 'Do you know why I ran away that time, Marianna, from your house?'

She shook her head. She did not know; no one knew even now, not even his mother.

'Well, I want to tell you about it, Marianna.'

And he began to tell the tale of his life, from when he was a child. He spoke very quietly, as though to himself, his face turned away from her and still held between his hands. It was as if he was at confession and his words were occasionally lost in a breath of air. Marianna watched him, and that pale face seemed lit in the darkness by a distant light. The things he told her were already known to her as events in which she had taken part herself; and yet they came across to her as mysterious: they seemed like adventures from some fantasy.

The family was poor, he told her, the father always frail because of an inoperable hernia, the teenage sisters unsuited to go into service because they were respectable people — and also because, being very pretty, once they were out of their own house they would immediately fall prey to some libertine. The mother wore herself out working to keep her family and conceal its private hardships from the outside world. And she too was unwell but pretended not to be, in order not to make her husband's sufferings worse. He, Simone, was the youngest in the family: the sisters had brought him up, always carrying him about in their arms, always laughing with him. But he grew, and they grew more than he did: they were growing old, in fact, the elder of his sisters, and no one wanted them because they were too beautiful and too poor. And the annual crops were miserable: the grain the exhausted father brought home was meagre, the oil from the small olive grove scant. Everything was sparse in the family shut away in its little courtyard as if in exile from the joys of the world.

The grown-up sisters no longer laughed: they sewed, eyes hidden beneath the headscarves pulled over their brows. They sewed coats made of leather as hard as their own fate, or embroidered shirts and waistcoats for bridegrooms, but never for their own. The earnings were thin, however; in their lives everything was thin.

A relative had taken the young boy Simone to live on his farm. This relative passed himself off as a wealthy man but he was only rich in appearance. He had vices, and debts, and the moneylenders gnawed away at his mind. A stout and jolly man on the outside, he could turn ferocious at times, no one knew why.

'I was ten years old but he spoke to me as if I was a full-grown man. "Simone," he used to say, "we have to be bold, act like men, not be timid like hares." And he made me run up and down rocky hillsides at the risk of breaking my bones to teach me to be agile and leap about so that I could escape if anyone was after me. On one occasion he took me right down to the bottom of a ravine and left me there. He was on his horse and he was back at the top in no time. He shouted down: "This will teach you how to climb and not be scared." And I scrambled up, and when I got to the top he wasn't there any more and I had to find my own way back. I didn't cry, no, but I could feel my heart swell with pride inside my chest. Then he died and the debts ate up all his possessions. My family had vainly been hoping for an inheritance. Then I was a shepherd, and I was alone, for years and years, quite alone, a farmhand, a servant. My skills, my agility were of no use. I went home and found my father on his sleeping mat, my mother exhausted and ill too, and my sisters embroidering clothes for other men to get married in. While they themselves never did get married. And as for me, I was eighteen, I hated men because they did not come for my sisters, and women because almost all of them had lovers and none of them paid any attention to my sisters. At that time I was working in your house. Yes, I hated you too because you were rich and could get married and they couldn't. I was grown up and I still thought childish things. I thought of locking you and your uncle in a room one night, of tying you up, of forcing you to give me all your money. But, God help me, your uncle's eyes terrified me. I can still see them now. And your housekeeper as well, always listening out for any strange noise, she made me think twice about things.

Once you sent me off on some journey, and I went to see my godfather, a well-to-do priest who lives in one of the villages. The excuse for going to him was to ask if he wanted to take me on as his servant, but in reality because I was hoping, I don't know, that he would take me into his household and leave me his inheritance, the way your uncle did for you. He welcomed me warmly enough, rot his guts, but he didn't want anything to do with me, not even as a servant. And that's how my youth was spent. I thought about going out robbing people to make my family rich. I would never have wanted to steal anything serious — not a lamb or an ox. Raid a few people who deserved it, yes — maybe get into my godfather's house and pinch his treasure. But not carry off a lamb, the way an eagle or a polecat does. But where were the companions I needed to go raiding? Those days are passed, Marianna, my Marianna! The disaster is that I used to go round telling everyone these things, and I got myself a bad name. People kept a close eye on me, watched out for me, spied on me — me, who never harmed a fly. And when I returned home, my mother just looked at me sadly and my father lectured me from his sleeping mat in a voice that seemed to come from beneath the earth. I told him: father, you're a living corpse, buried above ground because you've never had strength and courage, because you've lived like a hare afraid to come out of its form. My sisters were smiling under their headscarves, almost approving of me... and so, Marianna, and so one day I decided to change my life. I'll always remember it. It was winter, one of the Sunday festivals. I'd mingled with the people, all hidden behind their masks, but while everyone was enjoying themselves I was thinking of my sisters sitting sadly at home around the fire, and of my father leaning against the wall outside in the deserted alley. What was I good for if I couldn't manage to improve my family's miserable life? That night I was supposed to come back here to the sheep pens and instead I went off into the Orgosolo hills. At first I had no clear idea in mind; but I was thinking of joining forces with some outlaw or other and trying my luck with him. It was bound to be better than working as a servant all week and going back to my house to hear my father's sermons. I met Costantino Moro, my companion, who was trying to warm himself at a fire by the side of the road like a beggar. When he told me his troubles I laughed. By my faith as a Christian, he made me sorry for him. But to avoid remaining all alone, I stayed with him. And that is how, Marianna, I was immediately accused of a thousand crimes I hadn't committed. And I'd make the judge laugh if I told him so. But now, however... now...'

He fell silent, dropped his head again.

'Now,' he resumed after a short silence, 'now I would like to change my life again. But how, Marianna, how?'

'The way to do it would be...' Marianna began in hoarse voice, in whose tone she herself recognised the uncertainty and agitation; and she did not have the courage to go on.

Simone, however, understood straightaway what she was trying to suggest, and he seemed to wake up, to rebel against it. He gave her a sideways look, a look almost of hatred, then rose to his feet, shook himself vigorously, settling the cartridge belt round his waist and picking up his gun. Standing over her, he sought her eye again but she would no longer look at him. It seemed they were offering each other a rope to safety and were both of them jumping out of the way to avoid it.

'Well, anyway, everything's fine, so long as I don't lose my freedom,' he said, his voice emphatic. 'Everything, Marianna. The one thing I won't do is be a servant again. Forgive me for having told you so many stories. Goodbye, Marianna. Give me your hand.'

Marianna reached out a hand, raising her eyes. But this time it was Simone who would not meet them. He barely squeezed her fingers and strode off, without looking back. Still seated, her eyes followed him. She felt a sense of liberation and at the same time a sharp pain, a simultaneous surge of both self-respect and humiliation. It was as if her former servant had offended her by not relieving her of the status of mistress.

'Good luck,' she wished him privately, to herself, 'since we'll never see each other again.'

Deep down, however, she felt that he would be back.

After dinner she began to prepare for her return to Nuoro. She was due to leave at first light, yet late into the night she was still getting her things together, unable to decide to go to bed. She looked around the lonely little room, which enclosed her like a nest against the vague murmurings of the trees; and her big house in Nuoro, damp and dark, with its iron-braced door and solid windows, appeared before her like a prison. It even had its unrelenting warden, the housekeeper Fidela, with her keys on her belt and her eyes ever on the look-out. But then all of us are like that in this life: captives expiating the very guilt of being alive. We either resign ourselves or break down the walls, like Simone. The hour of liberation will come for all, and the recompense.

She sat on the doorstep, facing the east, thinking all these wise things. But she felt disturbed. There seemed to be more to be done in preparation for the return journey, something important that she had forgotten, the most important thing of all. She didn't know what it was.

The men were sleeping in the kitchen; all was silence; stars twinkled, grasshoppers sang, as on the evening of Simone's second visit. She wanted to go to sleep where she was, here on the threshold. She felt unsteady, like someone inebriated, after drinking so much new air these past days, so much of the soft warmth of spring.

She could see the tree in the middle of the silvery clearing and the dogs asleep in its shadow; and further off the two wings of the forest, bright on the side of the flowering holm oaks, dark on the side of the cork oaks; and between the two wings the empty distance pale in the shimmer of imminent moonrise, with the mountains beginning to show their outlines as if slowly approaching through a tremulous veil of light.

First was mount Oliena, white, made of air, then the Dorgali mountains to the right and the Nuoro ones to the left, blue and black; and then all at once the whole horizon seemed to blossom with golden clouds. It was the moon rising.

And suddenly, above the golden veil that stretched from the mountains to the Sierra, there appeared another veil, a net threaded with pearls which shimmered over all the rest and made everything still more beautiful, more alive in this dreamscape. The forest was laughing in the night, and yet the leaves which fell from the holm oaks seemed like tears. Nightingales were all about, singing. One was even in the tree in the clearing: with the singing of the bird, and the moon shining through the branches of the tree, the effect was of sound and light radiating from a single sphere.

Marianna dimly remembered how, as a child, she used to

watch for just such an effect on the night of the festival of San Giovanni. She would wait, in the dark courtyard of her house, for the heavens to open at midnight and let the face of God appear in the middle of a luminous garden.

She rose, half dazed. She heard the distant footsteps again, saw a man advancing across the clearing, small at first then growing taller, taller still, tall enough to touch the sky. She recognised Simone. So she sat down, rigid, waiting with something like fear.

She knew it, that he would come back. And she realised she had stayed out on the step to wait for him. Now, she would have liked to withdraw into the house and she was no longer able to. She seemed to see his eyes gleaming in the darkness under the golden moon, fixed on her with a look that pinned her to the stone step. And she seemed to see his hands reach out for her as on that first evening when they had tried to clutch the ground before her.

She started to get to her feet again. She was afraid; she knew perfectly well that two men were just nearby, ready to protect her; yet she seemed to be alone in the world, alone with the soft and terrible shadow which was silently advancing the way one saw things in dreams. And deep inside, she knew that no one could save her from the danger looming over her except herself.

But with the man's steady approach, she lost the last scraps of confidence in her own strength. Her knees folded, and when Simone took her hands and drew her up again, inviting her to come and sit, and himself sat cross-legged on the ground before her, without letting go of her hands, she suddenly felt like a different person, a thing belonging to him.

'My father is just in there,' she murmured.

Making no reply, Simone shook off his cap with a twist of the head and lowered his forehead into her lap, childlike and weary. His short thick hair, its little curls silvered by the moonlight, smelled of grass, of dust, of sweat, an odour both wild and aromatic which disturbed Marianna more than the gesture he made. She felt her heart melt. It seemed to her that he had laid his head in the lap as a token of himself, and she loved him like a sleeping child. She felt she had the power to protect him, to save him, to gather him into her very body like a son of her own.

She freed a hand from his grasp and stroked his forehead; without knowing it, she was crying; and the tears fell on his hair and sparkled like dew on grass. But the still moment, the sleeping moment passed: with a wriggle of the neck he tried to burrow his head deeper between her knees, and not succeeding, lifted it and pushed his face towards hers, eyes closed and lips apart, avid. Then, as she attempted to free herself he caught her two trembling hands again, clutching them as if with talons.

'Marianna,' he murmured, barely audible, yet menacing, beseeching; and then soft and hopeful he repeated: 'Marianna!'

He felt her shudder and then relax, trustfully abandoning her hands to him; and then he calmed down too; he did not repeat his attempt to kiss her, and began to speak, quietly, tonelessly, his head bent forward and hers, above, craning to hear him.

What was it? His voice, or the voice of this farmstead, animated by the nightingale's song, stirred by the breeze that accompanied the rising of the moon? This is the moment when every leaf shivers mournfully, it knows not why, perhaps because it cannot detach itself and fly, perhaps because one day it must detach itself and fall. And the swaying of the treetops and the soughing of the wind echo the movement and the murmur of the ocean, held back by every shoreline and flinging itself in vain against them from one end of the earth to the other.

'What are you afraid of, Marianna, when I'm here at your feet like a sick dog? Don't be afraid. If I wanted to harm you I wouldn't have come like this, at this hour of night, alone, unarmed. Don't you see I have no weapons? I don't even have the clasp-knife I had when I was little and went hunting lizards. I've left all my weapons down there by the spring. They can rust, I don't care. Who are you afraid of? Your father? If he saw us like this, loving each other, he would bless us. Your servant? He was the one who told me today you were going... so I came, today, and I've come back now... if I wanted to harm you I'd come with my companions and I'd tie you up like a lamb and carry you off over my shoulder and lay this place to waste if they didn't let me through... Marianna! I'm here, instead, you can see, I'm still your servant. I put my head in your lap and you can take it in your hands like the fruit of the chestnut tree which is all spines on the outside and inside as soft as bread...'

Marianna listened, bending ever lower, and it seemed as if she was inhaling a breath of untamed power from the heat, the smell of him. She felt proud to be loved like this, by a man like him, to have him at her feet. But what was good in it; and what was bad? Did there exist any difference between Simone and her; what could divide them? For long years they had been servants together; and now that they were free, their own masters, they were meeting again, and loved each other, as if in deliberate reaction against their former servitude.

'Marianna, hear me. I've been thinking about you all the time these last few days. The way you look at me, it's like a rope that's binding me. And don't think it was like this back in the old days, no. When I was your servant I didn't love you. On the contrary, I hated you, as I hated everyone. I hated you but I was also in awe of you, of your uncle with his stern eyes in that face of a carved saint, watching me, watching me. I used to see them all the time, and sometimes I still do. You were the masters, and I hate masters. But sometimes I thought: yes, I'd like it if I could marry Marianna, but not for her possessions, the way other men wanted her. At other times, instead, I told myself: if Marianna were to fall in love with me, and let me know it, I'd refuse her just to make her suffer! But even with all this, maybe yes, I liked you. I remember the two of us one day looking together down a well where something had fallen, and I felt you next to me and I saw our two faces at the bottom of the well. And it gave me the feeling that we were together somewhere in some distant place, away from the world. And it has happened. As God's my witness, it made me tremble all over. Even now it makes a deep impression when I think back to it. Do you remember it too?'

'Yes,' she said, in a sudden moment of recollection; and she shivered.

Simone squeezed her hands tighter, shaking her lightly to bring her back to the present.

'I shall never be able to marry you, Marianna. That's why I'm here: so that you won't think I'm like the others. I know I'm doing a bad thing by being here... but I couldn't not come.

It's as if I'm bewitched, Marianna, and may the Lord help me. Do you think I didn't try to go away that first evening, and the second, and every day, and today when I said goodbye? I've tried, but it's no good. Those first few nights I prowled round your farm as if there was a high wall and I couldn't find the opening. Several times I came as close as I could and I felt I could sense your breathing and that was enough. Have you seen how the dogs never even stirred? Because they know me and know that I love you, Marianna. But you're silent, Marianna, and you're right. What can you have to say to me? Nothing. And I am here, your servant, and you must no longer be afraid of anything. Not of anything, Marianna! Your possessions will be guarded by me as if by all the power of the law. Don't be afraid of anything. If your father were to come out here and catch me by surprise, I'd let him kill me, I'd let all my blood fall on your lap without complaint. But what are you doing now, Marianna, are you crying? Are you crying? A woman who loves me mustn't cry.

'And now you'll be thinking: why have I suddenly begun to love him? Because you've seen my eyes, Marianna, and behind my eyes my soul. And it's the same with me. We had never looked at each other. It's because we had never met before. But now we know each other. And perhaps you're thinking: I'm doing wrong to love him because he has taken things that belonged to other people and he has spilled Christian blood, and it's a sin to love him. That's what you think, but you don't believe it. Because your soul tells you that it just isn't true that I've done such terrible things.'

'Yes,' she said impulsively, 'that's right!'

Then he raised himself to his knees, without letting go of

her hands.

'You see me? I'm kneeling before you the way you kneel before Mary. You see me, Marianna? I'm not lying. I'm not vile; I've never done so many bad things that you couldn't love me.'

And even though their faces were almost touching, he did not kiss her. He bent his head again and crawled still closer to her, until her feet were trapped between his knees, and for a while he remained like that, looking up at her, breathing heavily.

'And yet, listen to me,' he went on after a moment. 'I have this hope, that I will be the one to put the wedding ring on your finger. If you'll wait for me, I will be your husband, Marianna Sirca, remember that. It's why I've made a vow not even to kiss you, you see, because I respect you as the woman who must come to me virgin and pure. Promise you'll wait for me — but first, be mindful of what you're promising, Marianna!'

'I honour any promise I make,' she said, quiet and serious again. 'You don't know me yet, Simone!'

'I know you, woman!' he protested. 'I have known you for a long time, since the first day I set foot in your house. Did you think me just a boy? I was a hundred years old and I could read people's souls in their eyes. Listen, you made me feel both pity and rage. I hated you but I knew you. You were what I was, a servant and nothing else. You too were there as a servant out of pity for your family, so as not to be a burden to your father and your mother. And the wealth around you was not yours any more than it was mine. And this is it, Marianna! For a long time we were dull and thoughtless; we were like children who aren't allowed to touch anything. But now we are the masters, yes, us, and we'll do whatever we want.'

Marianna smiled, a little disbelieving. To conceal her smile she bent forward until her mouth just brushed his hair. And the contact was enough to send a shudder surging through him from his heels to the nape of his neck, but he controlled himself again.

'Listen to me, Marianna. I can't properly tell you what I'll do, but you must trust me. I will come to your house one night, in Nuoro, I can't tell you exactly when, but certainly before Christmas. And you'll be expecting me. If you don't see me by then, it means I'm dead! If I do come though, it will be with some good news. Don't get tired of waiting, and if they say bad things about me, don't believe them. Above all, don't be afraid. And now, let me go.'

He dropped her hands, but remained bent towards her, with his face on her knees, and it seemed that he was recovering his strength before undertaking the mysterious journey towards the good things which had been ordained.

'What is he going to do?' Marianna wondered.

Even though she had such faith in him it made her heart tremble, she could only see one sure way to turn the dream into reality. And so she found the strength to open her mind to him frankly.

'Simone, hear me out: if you have committed no crimes, as you say and as I believe, well then… Simone, why don't you hand yourself over to the authorities? You'll be acquitted or given only a light penalty. After that, we'll have all the happiness that is to come. Yes, I will wait for you.'

And as after a violent exertion, she felt her knees tremble. Her promise frightened her, but she did not regret it. Tears of sweetness and anguish returned and filled her eyes; and through their iridescent veil she seemed to see a rainbow curving from one border of her lands to the other, and she remembered how when she was a little girl she used to go in search of the ring — the ring of happiness — in the spot where the rainbow rose or came to earth.

And it was this ring then, that Simone was promising her. He, however, seemingly coming back to life, caught one of her hands again, lifted it to his face, and drew on it the sign of the cross.

'Marianna,' he said, standing up, not answering her question, 'don't cry. You promised not to cry. Farewell; and wait for me.'

III

He walked until dawn was breaking, making for Mount Gonare, whose peak he could clearly see rising like a pyramid, blue under the moon amid the grey outlines of the other mountains.

His movements were agile, his step light. The muzzle of the gun slung over his shoulder gleamed like a silver ring.

Now, yes, he seemed high enough to touch the moon — as he had dreamed when he was a little boy and gazed, feverish and starving, at the flocks of sheep other people owned. Everything was there, below him, and he could grasp it and fling it down at his feet at the flick of a finger.

He had become one of the masters, as he had longed to be when he was bound in servitude. Marianna, his mistress in those days, the woman who never even looked him in the face, Marianna loved him and had promised to wait for him. How had all this happened? Hardly had he seen her up there in the hills, sitting outside her little farmhouse in the very places where he had been a servant, ill-treated by the other servants, before all his violent desires of those times had returned, and all finding their embodiment in her. To seize her was to seize all the things she represented. And so he had remained on watch in the woods around her, like a hunter. But all the time he watched, he was thinking how best to catch her: alive and not dead, in a way that allowed him to possess her for ever and not just for a moment.

And so he had fallen at her feet, instead of attacking her, and now he was glad to have done so, to be one half of a pair, like that image at the bottom of the well. A pair? He stopped abruptly, turned round, cast a long look towards the dark scrubland of the Sierra.

And a throbbing filled his chest.

At first it was desire for the woman, then regret at not having taken her there and then. Were they really a pair? But if she was so far away, as ungraspable as that reflection in the well...? And he felt something rise within him, like a wild beast that slept deep in his entrails. It seemed suddenly to wake, sending a jolt through his whole body and making him leap. A howl of hunger and of pain rang out inside him, filling his ears with its roaring and his eyes with blood.

He dropped to the ground, face down, squirming, pressing his breast and stomach against the earth to crush the beast and force it back into its lair: he needed to prevent it from urging him to retrace his steps, go back and simply take Marianna, even if it meant blood and death.

When the convulsion had passed, he righted himself, but remained sitting on the grass, running his hands wildly through his hair; then he sniffed his fingers and caught the scent of Marianna on them. He began to speak to her again, his voice submissive, his chest still throbbing from the fierce battle with himself.

'You'll see, I'll do you no harm, Marianna, you'll see. You must rest easy, and stay firm. And I... I shall go, wherever fate takes me, as God dictates, and I will make my fortune at all costs, yes, even if I have to go to the rainbow's end.'

He set off again. He had no idea what he would do, where the fortune he sought was to be found. For now, he was making his way to the refuge where he had left his partner, and more than anything he wanted to reach the safety of his hideaway and think things through.

He walked and walked: he knew all the places, all the tracks and paths, as well as he knew the palm of his hand. Just before dawn he arrived at the refuge, halfway up the slopes of Mount Gonare looking towards the valleys of Olzai. It was a place with its own kind of fearful beauty: a cave with two openings, one of which gave out on to a rising scree of rocks, over which it was easy to escape in case of pursuit. To arrive at the cave one had to weave through a labyrinth of boulders, stones, scrubby bushes and wild-growing trees. Among the oaks, twisted and contorted by centuries of winds, rocks stuck up here and there like diabolical heads; then a wood of rough and stunted holm oaks formed a dense barrier round the cave. But once up there, from a kind of niche hollowed out in the boulders, he could look out across the whole panorama of the valley.

After scanning with an eagle eye the solitude all around, he went into the cave. The ash-covered fire, a piece of raw meat in a recess and a thin cord attached to a peg in the wall told him that his absent companion would be back soon. From the signs of the disturbed bushes at the front of the cave, and from the ashes still smoking with animal fat and the bones scattered about, it was clear however that other men had been here, feasting themselves and maybe plotting, and he became anxious. He trusted his companion like a brother, but his naivety left him uneasy.

So he returned to the niche above the rock, his gun at his side, and waited watchfully.

He saw the sky lighten, and through the bushes the shining mirror of a shell-shaped pool where the water from a spring gathered. This spring, after tumbling down from the boulders above the cave, seemed to halt at a bed of flowering reeds to rest, like himself, before running on its way.

The moon was sinking over the pool as if about to plunge into it, attracted by the soft reflections of its own light.

And the moon appeared to revel in the fading night, free and alone in the deserted spaces of the dawn sky above the still sleeping land. It hid, it reappeared between the reed stems, it gazed at its reflection in the water, shimmering with a thousand smiles, taking pleasure in seeing itself naked, free and alone.

But even the moon was being drawn towards its fate by something inevitable, pulling it down; and it turned paler at the knowledge and grew sad and cold, and even its smile in the water's reflections began to die. It tried to delay by hiding among the branches of a holm oak, as if the tree offered refuge; soon however it had to sink further; it clung to the projecting spur of a boulder and held on for a moment, though already weary and pale; then suddenly it let go of the spur as well and seemed to drop all at once and eventually fall free like a flower losing its petals.

Everything then gave a sigh, in the silvery penumbra of the dawn; the breathing of the water among the reeds was answered by the breathing of the leaves. The day was stirring in solitude. Simone, by contrast, felt himself drawn down like the moon by the sweet pull of sleep. And he too fought against it. And Marianna was with him, kissing him; but among the boulders enemies were watching and he could not afford to lose himself in thoughts of sleep and of love.

And so everything turned red, after the silver of dawn, then everything turned gold and blue; and the wind tossed the trees against the sky; little white summer clouds glided overhead, hawks and kites; the sun had climbed halfway up in the sky and the pool of water now reflected its entire body.

At last reassured, Simone rose to his feet and scrambled back down to the cave.

He relit the fire, threaded the meat on the wooden spit and set it to roast over the flame; finally he took off all his clothes and went down, naked, to the pool, glancing at his pale chest, as white as a woman's.

His eyes constantly looked around while he rubbed his feet with tufts of maidenhair fern which left a greenish tinge on the skin; when he lifted his head to listen to the distant noises, his handsome eyes reflected the green and gold surrounding him; he shivered, and across his white back, which was freckled with large black moles, the shadows of the reeds trembled.

He rose and tested the bottom of the pool with one foot. And so, little by little, he edged forward and submerged himself in the water, even his head, which he abruptly jerked up again and shook, sending brilliant droplets from his hair.

And suddenly he became light-hearted, confident; everything around him was beautiful; golden lilies shone like small flames among the reeds; bright cobwebs shimmered on frail threads between one flower and the next. A nightingale was singing and it seemed as if it was the spring's tumbling water that purled from its throat.

Crouching in the pool, he scrubbed his skin thoroughly, but every now and then bounced up to look at his chest and arms, whose hairs glittered with pearly drops. Then he crouched in the water again and tried in vain to catch some little brown trout between his palmed hands as they slid by, carried on the current.

'But I'll catch them for you, Marianna!' he shouted, surprising himself and setting off an echo. 'Marianna! Marianna!'

Then he shouted his own name too: 'Simone! Simone!' childishly imagining it was she, answering him.

So the hours passed and evening came again, with the moon and the great sighing of the air which brought a mysterious kind of transformation to things. The profiles of the rocks on the mountain crests looked like human faces turned upwards to contemplate the sky. The stars stood close over them but remained unable to decide to touch them. Everything was suspended, in its stillness, everything was waiting, eager for something which seemed imminent but never came.

Simone had dozed for a long time after his bath and his meal, and was now back in the niche above the cave, waiting for his partner. He was calmer now, but simultaneously more disturbed by thoughts of Marianna.

'This time last night we were together...' And he could picture himself burying his face between her knees and he felt a desire to bite them. 'What an idiot I was! But as far as Costantino is concerned, I'll tell him I kissed her. And here he is now, thank God, he's coming up. What a slow devil he is.'

He could recognise his step, cautious but not agile and sure-footed like his own, and one that annoyed him every time he heard it. In point of fact, everything about Costantino jarred, especially when it came to moving about, to working together as a pair. They were like two little brothers who love each other well enough but question how long it can go on, and the elder tyrannises the younger but is also his protector. Here he comes now, Costantino: a small figure, peaceful as a hare-trapper, with his gun slung across his jacket of greenish velvet. A black-fringed fur cap gives his ruddy face with its prominent cheekbones a second head of disordered curls. The wide mouth, half open to reveal the big teeth, seems to smile continuously, but the slanting eyes are sad and sullen beneath the black fringe of the cap pulled low over his forehead.

He sat in the cave and began to unlace his boots by the light of the moon, not responding to the ironic questions addressed to him by Simone, who had jumped to his feet and now sat down opposite him.

'Costantì! Nice to see you! Have you been to a festival? Have you been meeting your young lady?'

Still not answering, Costantino threw himself back and lay full length on the ground; he was panting. His partner touched his hand and it was burning hot; so he changed his tone.

'What is it? Are you feverish? Where have you been and who's been here?'

Costantino seized his hand and held on to it.

'Why did you leave me here alone?' he complained. 'Why?'

'Am I your mother then? Do I have to spoon-feed you?'

'Three people came looking for you, two older men and a young one. They wanted to see you very badly. Go and look for him, I said, what do you want me to do, make a carving of him for you? He went away on Friday and I don't know where he is. They went away, they came back, they brought a sheep and some wine. They waited for you. From what they were saying, but especially what the young fellow told me, I understood they wanted you to go with them to rob a country priest, a rich priest who owns lots of gold and silver plate. He's the parish priest in a village but he keeps the stuff hidden at his mother's place on a sheep farm. She's an old lady and he goes to spend a few days with her from time to time. Well, Simone, when you didn't come back, those three took it out on me. What are you doing here, sexton? they said. Minding my own business. And they laughed at me and said, we don't know how Simone Sole can bear your company. Clear off, take a bag and go and beg for alms with the beggars at the country fairs. They ended up making me angry. You know I never get angry, Simone, but when I do get angry I get angry. They got scared of me and went away. But for a moment I thought they'd come back and kill me. So I went away as well.'

Now it was Simone who made no response, sitting very still, leaning forward to listen, staring intently at his partner. He found his story very odd, and incomplete in some way.

'No,' he said in the end, 'you're hiding something, Costantì! Open your eyes and look at me: where have you been?'

Costantino propped himself on one elbow and looked him in the eyes.

'What's it to you? And anyway, where have you been?'

He fell back, his head against his arm, and closed his eyes. Costantino was a man who could be suspicious and honourable in equal measure, and Simone, remembering he had to deal with him either brutally or gently, lay down beside him and lightly touched his foot with his own.

'I'll tell you where I've been, yes, why shouldn't I? But you speak first. What were those three like?'

And when Costantino had given him a good description of them, he smiled, flattered.

'Now I know who they are. The younger man is Bantine Fera: I knew he'd eventually want to find me.'

Costantino opened his eyes again, suspicious and jealous: he knew who this Bantine Fera was, a bandit, very young, younger even than Simone, and bolder, more independent, ready for anything. His partner had talked about him many times, and even now he began to sing his praises again, though not without a faint degree of envy.

'There's a fellow who's sure to make his fortune. I heard that the Corraine gang asked him to go with them, because he's a good shot; he's good at everything; he can pluck birds out of the air. And then he's not afraid of anything: he's only risking his own skin, after all, as he hasn't got a mother or sisters, like us. He's a bastard, born out of wedlock, anything's easy for him. Still, God help me, I'm pleased he came to look for me.'

'You said he'd had bad words for you, he made fun of you.'

'Of me? No one has ever made fun of me, Costantì! Hold your tongue. Being good with a gun and slaughtering people on the roadside gives no one the right to make fun of Simone Sole! Or maybe the bastard boy only did it when he was with you?'

'No,' said Costantino, who was a man of conscience and never told lies. 'He didn't make fun of you. But perhaps I made fun of him. Anyway, yes, when the three of them had gone, I disappeared myself, and I went right up into the hills, to the sheep pastures, to warn the priest, because you can rob anyone you like, but not a priest, no. Anyway, yes,' he continued, eyes closed but peaceful at last, 'I ran for two nights and when I got there it was just the white-haired old lady, white as a dove. Give me something to drink, I said, I'm a thirsty traveller. And when she'd given me something to drink I warned her of the danger the farm was in, and I left. And even if your Bantine came now and beat me up, or picked me off from a distance with his gun, my conscience would be at peace, it's the only thing I've got left. But a priest, no, a priest shouldn't be robbed.'

'Costantino Moro, do you know what I ought to say to you? Neither you nor I are suited to being bandits. We were born as pure as church wardens and we shall die the same simple souls.'

'Go to hell, go and knock on the hangman's door,' Costantino swore under his breath. But his curses seemed more directed at certain absent persons, perhaps the three criminals who had harassed him.

Simone, meanwhile, was not sure whether he was pleased or displeased with what had happened. He certainly didn't like the idea of cutting a weak figure in comparison to Bantine Fera, and at the same time he approved of Costantino, who, by his very weakness in alerting the priest, had shown he cared nothing for the young outlaw's bullying.

On the other hand, the job the three men had proposed was a good one and easy too, and he understood Bantine Fera's purpose in suggesting they do it together. He was offering an alliance, an association, and Simone was feeling increasingly flattered by it.

All at once vanity filled his heart with joy and pride.

'Well, I certainly won't go looking for him if he doesn't come back,' he said, as if to himself. 'But I need... I need...'

'What do you need?'

'Costantino, tell me where this priest's farm is.'

Costantino did not speak again. He understood what his companion was thinking. And he did not regret having spoken out, but he felt a deep sadness; and more than sadness at Simone's intention, which he had guessed, there was envy and jealousy of Bantine Fera's potency, and above all that there was a feeling of loneliness, of the distance that separated him from everyone, whether far or near.

In his turn, Simone felt that Costantino had penetrated his thoughts and was disturbed by his companion's discernment. It made him irritable and he tried to conceal it by speaking; and in speaking he was concealing from himself his real self, so that he listened to his own words and believed them true.

'Costantì! Yes, I want to go up to that farm by myself, even if just to make it clear it wasn't me who sent you! I need money, do you understand? Why do I have to let the opportunity slip? I need money, Costantì. Something has happened to me. I've met a woman and I need money... you don't believe me?' He went on after a moment's painful silence. 'It doesn't matter whether you believe me or not. It's a fact, and that's enough. The woman is rich, she's beautiful — as beautiful as any woman, and owns everything around her. As rich as all your relations put together,' he insisted, increasingly irritated by Costantino's immobility. 'Just from the sale of the cork from her woods she collects a thousand *scudi* a year. Her farmhouse has its value too. Yes, well anyway, it's Marianna Sirca, the woman who once had power over me as the master's daughter. She's loved me from the time I was a servant in her house. But she wasn't mistress of her own affairs, then; and in any case I was very proud with her. Now, we've understood each other: God has willed it this way. The night before last we were together at her farm, we were together even though her father was there. We were together,' he repeated, closing his eyes also and becoming agitated, 'and I kissed her.'

Costantino did not immediately reply. He could feel his heart beating against the hard ground. In the end, since Simone remained silent, seemingly lost in recollection, he asked jokingly: 'And that's the reason why you need money, is it? You have to marry her?'

'I can marry her, yes, if I want to! It's what she wants, in fact, because she's not like other women.'

'What sort of woman is she? If she was a serious woman she wouldn't pay any attention to you.'

Then Simone half rose, fierce with anger.

'If you say another word about her I'll smash your head in with your own boots. Understood?'

Costantino was unafraid. He straightened himself too, and

sat with his elbow on his knee and his chin on his hand, gazing into the fire. And when he saw Simone lie down again, he said thoughtfully: 'Simone, you're not talking like a man any more. How can someone like you marry a woman like that?'

'How? Before a priest, for heaven's sake, in secret. And then, no one says I have to spend my whole life running round the country like a wild animal. I can even come back as a free man.'

'Ah, you see, you've gone soft already. The woman's already moulded you in her own image. And she's bewitched you too. Fine; but mind you don't lose your identity altogether, *man*!'

'You're talking like that because you envy me, you're jealous. You're afraid of being left alone!'

'Me?' Costantino said, raising sad eyes. And he rapidly smiled and shook his head in a gesture borrowed from Simone, with a little sideways twist of the neck. 'I can always give myself up. That way I'd be able to join you in the dock.'

'Well damn you, then, you with all your sins. Who's talking of standing in any dock?'

'And how do you mean to go back as a free man without a trial and all those legal debates? And you'll end up before the judge; and you'll get yourself clapped in irons and never free your feet from the shackles. Plead guilty? Is that what the woman advised you?'

'It's true,' Simone said, and felt an undefined terror.

It was true, it was all true, yes: sometimes he did feel bewitched. Marianna dominated him; he felt her weight pressing on his shoulders. And he felt ashamed that even Costantino could guess it. He leapt up, as if he wanted to shake the woman off, and flapped his cap at the burning fire since even the fire seemed to be murmuring against him. And the flames wavered as if trying to dodge away in fright, but soon they rose again, higher than before, murmuring more powerfully.

'Our fate can't be avoided,' Costantino said. 'You are a different man from the one you were three days ago: your fate is sealed.'

'No, Costantì, I'd sooner God cut off both my legs! I swear to you on these flames, I swear on my mother's heart, I will never give myself up. I haven't the slightest intention of getting married; not in public and not in secret either. It was just a manner of speaking. If she wants me, she must have me as I am!'

'She won't have you, not the way you are!'

'Then I'll have her!' he said with bravado.

But soon he too leant his elbow on his knee and propped his chin on his hand; and they remained like that for a long time, the pair of them, as if suspended in limbo, listening to the faint whisperings and stirrings around their rocky den; big and ferocious like beasts lying in wait, small and nervous like chicks in the nest.

IV

Marianna was at her house in Nuoro again.

Lying in her large and freshly-made bed and overcome by a pleasant weariness, she imagined herself, as she drifted towards sleep, still up at the farmhouse, sitting on the step, with Simone's head in her lap. And she was speaking to the young man, softly, in a calm and serious manner, saying all the things she had not known how to say to him the night before. And she found herself bold enough to stroke his smooth warm hair, and the contact made her shudder from head to toe. Even her eyelids quivered, but she shut them firmly to prevent herself from crying, and from waking up.

'A woman who loves a man such as me must not cry... yes, yes, Simone, I mustn't cry.'

And she lay there motionless, with the feeling that her wrists were bound with cord and her feet with chains: and even if years were to pass, she would not have moved, for the cord was him, the chains were him.

This was love, then. An agitation hidden deep in the heart, and an enslavement to that agitation. Yet it was a sweet delight to go to sleep like this, bound, with a secret of her own within her heart.

Waking early the next morning, she experienced the uncertain joy of the prisoner who counts off the days of his sentence, knowing that they must eventually reach an end. One day may be just beginning but another is already gone, and each moment is a step towards freedom.

'At Christmas, if not before…'

Christmas will come: she is accustomed to long months of solitude and silence. And there was a time when she had no expectations of anything else, when she imagined nothing new would ever happen for her. Now, instead, the days seemed full of expectation, of hope: days and months were there on her fingertips, light as the petals of a flower. At Christmas Simone will come! And what if he didn't come? What if the wild and dangerous life he had adopted were to take him away for ever, to separate them again?

At this thought, she jumped up, ran to open the window, feeling she was suffocating.

The low window, made from four small panes, looked out at the rear of the house on to kitchen gardens and dark huts beyond which, on the sharp horizon, rose the rocky peaks of mount Orthobene.

The rosy light of dawn illuminated the large, low room with its yellow-washed wooden ceiling. The mirror of a new wardrobe shone beside the antique chest with its primitive decorations of birds and flowers. And Marianna moved away from the window to face her wide wooden bed, turning her back on the far wall to avoid glimpsing herself half naked in the mirror.

But in getting dressed she found her eyes drawn against her will by the movements of her image reflected in the glass. And she turned, just for a moment, glancing at herself with timid curiosity. Yes: it was a different woman who inhabited her bedroom now, a living and beautiful woman. The old Marianna had been left up there on the farm, buried beneath the dead leaves of the holm oaks. Why shouldn't she look at herself? She turned round resolutely and examined herself, with a curiosity entirely chaste and modest, as though she were examining a statue. Above the long, smooth lower legs she saw two little knees, pale and shiny like fruits made of polished marble; and she ran the palms of her hands over them, then bent to put on her shoes. The unfastened tresses of her hair slid like black snakes from her shoulders to fall across a white breast veined with purple. She threw them back with one hand while with the other she paused for a moment to stroke the pinkish curve of her arched heel. But suddenly she blushed, and darted towards the window again where she set about restoring order to her hair, smoothing it down properly on her forehead so that it resembled a bandage of black velvet, hardly divided by the white line of a parting. The scents from the kitchen gardens and the silence of the early hour reminded her of the farmstead; and here was Simone again, crouched at her feet, pressing her knees together, preventing her from moving. And yet she had to move, to take up and repair the broken thread of her old life. She bent towards him, as it seemed, to tell him: 'Simone, you have to let go of me, just a little.' He would not let her go, he was following her, clinging to her, so that it felt as though she was carrying him round with her, like a small child in her arms, showing him for a second time the house where he had once been a servant and was now becoming the master.

Here was the landing at the top of the steep slate staircase, quite dark between two bare white walls, with a floor of ancient flaking tiles. Off the landing stood the doors to the bedrooms, yellow with damp. All the rooms were damp, because of the big pergola that covered the courtyard between the house and the street. The lime-plastered walls were stained with green and the wooden ceilings were rotting, despite frequent renovations. Only the kitchen on the ground floor, with its window overlooking a kitchen garden to the east and the door to the courtyard, was warm and cheerful, since here, there was always a fire burning in the hearth.

When Marianna went down, the housekeeper had already gone out. The coffee was boiling over the embers in the hearth and the light of the rising sun shone on the copper pans hanging on the dark walls. Through the grille covering the window, the tufty heads of reeds quivered in the garden and further on, amongst white rose bushes sparkling with dew and low cherry trees hung with clusters of fruit like little coral castanets, a robin was flitting about uttering its lively alarm call.

Marianna pulled open the panels of glass and shook the rusting iron grille, almost as if trying to escape. Yes, Simone was right in not wanting to give up his freedom: anything, except his freedom!

But beyond the garden, in the alley that ran alongside it

and emerged on to the street in front of the house, a sound of horse's hooves rang out. The barrel of a gun and the tip of a cap showed over the wall. She recognised Sebastiano, and again the sense of reality caused her to blush. She hoped her relative would pass by. But instead he stopped and knocked at the street door by kicking at it with his foot. Without haste, she crossed the courtyard still kept in the shade by the pergola and opened the door. And at once she saw that Sebastiano was looking down at her, forcing his expression into its usual teasing smile, behind which the eyes, however, were suspicious and in truth sad as well.

'I wanted to know if Berte has gone.'

'Yes, he went back yesterday.'

'And how about you, Marianna: did you sleep well last night?'

'I always sleep well.'

'I know… you don't have thoughts to keep you awake! But… what was I going to say? Yes: the country air has done you good.'

Marianna sent him a long stare, waiting for some caustic remark. But he merely gazed ahead along the deserted street and without further ado flicked the reins and rode off, giving her a sad little wave.

'God be with you, Marianna. Goodbye.'

She stood in the doorway until the horse turned the corner of the street. She had the impression Sebastiano had already guessed her secret and was keeping an eye on her and watching over her the way one watches over someone threatened by some danger or illness. For a second, she was afraid of him, afraid of herself; but suddenly she twitched with irritation, thinking once again that she was mistress of herself and of her destiny, that she had been the servant of others long enough and no longer needed to account for anything to anyone.

And as if to prove to herself that she was free and alone, she continued to stand there on the threshold, a thing she had never done before, looking up and down the empty street. On a slight slope, it twisted down between buildings little better than hovels and ancient houses with wooden galleries and rusty iron balconies. And upwards, beyond the side alley, it opened out into a wider space with some greenery and the towers of the cathedral standing tall against the clear morning sky. No one came by; in the distance she could hear only the rumbling of a cart and the cry of a cockerel. Finally a woman appeared at the top of the street, with a milk canister in her hand, and Marianna realised she had stayed where she was exactly for this, to demonstrate to her servant that the moment of freedom had come. Indeed, even from a distance she could see the thick grey eyebrows bend in a frown above the elderly eagle's round eyes, but she did not retreat. The woman quickened her pace; her heavy shoes rang on the paved roadway like the iron-clad hooves of a horse, and her whole person, tall, hard, laced into its barbarous old costume, had something iron-grey and arrogant about it, old already but still indomitable.

'What are you staring at?' she asked her mistress, almost bumping her aside as she brushed past.

'I was with Sebastiano,' she replied; and saw suspicion immediately light up in her eyes.

'At this hour of the day? What did he want?'

'He wanted to rob me!' she said, laughing, while the servant shut the door and turned the key.

Once she was satisfied the door was securely locked and Marianna inside, calmly and silently at her work, the servant asked no further questions. She too set about her tasks, equally silent, except for the heavy tread of her footsteps all over the house making the floors shake.

And indeed, here she is, after putting the bedrooms in order, sitting on the floor in the room next to the kitchen, sieving the barley flour to make bread for the men up in the sheepfolds.

The sounds of sieving act as a kind of soporific on Marianna, seated too, by the window, sewing. Her thoughts are miles away. Instead of the reeds and little cherry trees of the kitchen garden, there stretch before her eyes the forests of the Sierra and the blue-tinted mountains; and life seems to her a dream. To shake herself out of it, she rises from time to time and goes out into the courtyard, walks towards the well and without meaning to, stares down into it. But it is her image alone that is reflected in its rounded surface, metallic, motionless and polished as a mirror. He is no longer there, or even anywhere near; he is in a place more profound and mysterious still.

Marianna comes back inside and casts an eye over the servant's work. The servant, in turn, has raised her head to check on her, and seeing that the door has not been opened and the mistress has not left the house, she carries on with her task. If it were not for the movement of her long arms, shaking the sieve inside a wide basket made of tightly-woven asphodel stems, she would resemble, covered as she is in fine flour right up to her bonnet, a stone statue whitened by a light shower of sleet.

And Marianna returns to her high stool beside the window; but the hours pass slowly; never have they seemed so long. She gets up again and goes to her room, and opens the chest and sees all her things tidily arranged. But the corseted waistcoat, neatly folded, with its sleeves laid out flat and silver buttons lying one on top of the other, and the tunic, also neatly laid out, with its pleats drawn together, its red border at the bottom, give her the impression of a dead Marianna, laid out in the coffin, ready for burial.

The entire past seemed like that, dead, cut cleanly out of life like the dead branch of a tree. She closed the chest and went into the other bedrooms; but in all of them, beginning with the late Canon's, with its bed still covered by the green counterpane, the priest's portrait hanging above the chest of drawers, the books behind the ground-glass panes of the bookcase, there hung the oppressive odour of things shut away, damp, underground.

Then she went up into the attic. It was a vast room spread out under the sloping roof, but still quite high, with two small windows which looked down over the courtyard and the street and from where one could see the gardens, the valley and the mountains. Bunches of grapes hung from the rafters, and strings of pears; on the floor, golden almonds and potatoes still as yellow as apples were laid out in boxes; there were also all the different breads: grey barley loaves for the farm-hands, black bread for the servant, white bread for her; and the flour and pasta, and the vegetables and all the provisions that are kept in an honest house. Nothing was lacking. And finally, in a corner between the two little windows, there was the servant's truckle bed, a low little platform with a worm-eaten wooden frame, and on it a coarse blanket of grey and black wool looking like a tiger skin.

Marianna sat there, her head filling with memories. The fragrant air flowed from one window to the other, and the blue sky over mount Orthobene was visible, with a little cloud floating in it, as pink as blossom. Distant voices echoed in the silence, and it seemed she could hear once more the voices of the farmstead. Yet she was drawn back to relive her past, remembering the day when her father and her mother had taken her by the hand and led her to her uncle's house and shown her the bedrooms, the staircase and this same attic, full of the Lord's bounty. Then too, she had sat on the drab little bed, touching the rough blanket with her little brown hand, thinking that she would never again play barefoot in the street, never again go to the fountain in the evenings with the other children, never again be able to utter bad words and blasphemies except to herself, under her breath. Farewell, freedom: now she had to wear shoes at all times, new, heavy shoes that seemed to drag her legs down, make them longer, clamp her feet to the floor, forcing her to consider every step.

In the early days, the servant Fidela had entertained her with her stories and her strange ways. She could see herself now, huddled in the bed with the servant's great hard feet pressing into her back. With so many beds in the house, large and small, with so many empty rooms, Fidela still wanted to sleep up here, and explained why.

'You have to understand that here, if there's a noise, you can look out and see all round the house.'

Indeed, she often got up in the night and leant out of one window or the other. Marianna, anxious, half-rising in the bed, would follow her with burning eyes when there was moon enough to make her out in the gloom; and she could dimly see her, quite naked but with her night bonnet on, looking big and solid like a wooden statue that moves about by the workings of some magical power. And Marianna was afraid, she was afraid of everything, of the servant on watch at the window, of the noises from outside, especially if they were not regular but suddenly rang out at odd moments; afraid of the objects she could just make out in the far depths of the attic, of the dark clusters hanging like untidy heads from the angled rafters. She was afraid of everything; and yet her fears were also pleasures. And in the daytime, when she was bored or was obliged to stand before her uncle, eyes lowered, in a state of uncertainty, she thought joyfully of those night hours, of the mysterious life of the attic, of the servant's stories.

'Tell me about it, tell me about it! When you were in that house, with those people as your masters, what was it like? What was it like...? Tell me, or I'll jump out of bed,' she would say, pushing back the blanket, when Fidela herself came up to bed.

'Well now... wait... what was I saying? But keep still, you little grasshopper!'

'Start again at the beginning. Hold my feet, Fidela!'

Fidela held her little feet between her stony knees and began again.

'So the thing you have to know is that when I was fifteen or sixteen, or maybe eighteen, I don't exactly know, I was a servant in the house of Cristina Zandu. They were rich, my master and mistress; so is the master here, may God be his comfort now, but they were rich too. They even had a fresh water fountain inside the house. And money and silver things and relics like in a church. And even, just inside the door, a trunk containing money, in coins, all lined up in a basket like rows of beans. Well, I can't exactly tell you how it happened, but anyway one evening, the evening of some festival, the master returned home with his big stick and went off to bed without stopping to eat any dinner, perhaps he'd been drinking. I couldn't swear to it, in all conscience, but he may have been drinking. We women were in the kitchen. The manservant was feeding the horses when, look, we saw him running back with his eyes wide in terror, shouting: "Oh mother! Oh, my mistress, what a fright! What a fright!" And he fled straightaway up a ladder that led to a lumber room above the kitchen; and I fled right behind him, my hair standing on end in terror, even though I'd no idea what it was about. And he promptly pulled the ladder up. Then he propped it against the wall, climbed up, smashed his way through the roof and disappeared. I had fallen to the floor of this lumber room and through a crack I saw the horrible thing that happened in the kitchen. A mob of masked men looking like ogres had burst in, and three of them had seized my mistress and one of them had a hatchet! The rest went straight into the passage and from there up into the bedrooms. You could hear their footsteps just like wild demons let loose from hell. Have you understood: they were a band of highwaymen? There were hordes of them, maybe thirty, maybe more. The manservant, out on the roof, was shouting for help, but no one dared show themselves for fear of attracting a hail of bullets. In a few minutes they killed the master and took all the valuable things — and they weren't satisfied with that. The one who had the hatchet, along with the two others, hauled the mistress round the house, dragging her as if she was a corpse, to make her tell them all the places where the money was hidden. Two gunshots rang out: it was the people from the house next door, trying to scare the robbers away. But some of them who'd stayed out in the courtyard on guard shouted back to the others inside: "Take no notice! Keep looking!" And the whole house was turned upside down as if there'd been an earthquake. I saw the three of them bring the mistress back into the kitchen. Her two feet were trailing behind her like rags and her face was all white and distorted with terror. They punched her in the back and threatened her with the hatchet, because she hadn't been able to tell them the hiding places. Then they undressed her. They found two banknotes on her, sewn into her bodice, a thousand lire each, and that seemed to calm them down. She was stammering: "For pity's sake, think of your mothers!" And they kept saying: "Just a little bit more. You're going to tell us where the cash is, or we'll put the pot-stand over the fire and make you sit on it naked." And one of them actually did put the metal tripod into the flames to heat it up. But then other gunshots were heard from outside and suddenly they all ran off. And my mistress too, when she found herself alone, she fled as well. I stayed up there all night. I hid between the bundles of reeds that were kept in the lumber room and sometimes even now I think I'm there, I think I can hear the robbers' footsteps all over the house, I feel I'm dying of suffocation. After that night, out of pure fright, I ceased to be a woman.'

This conclusion used to amuse Marianna greatly and made her laugh, despite her throat still being constricted with terror. She imagined she could see Fidela hidden between the bundles of reeds, in the lumber room, suddenly leaping out, transformed from a girl into a boy. And every time she waited anxiously for the end of the story, quivering with fear and pity, and simultaneously biting her lips so as not to laugh before the climax.

'Afterwards, I was the Canon's housekeeper. He'd become a parish priest up in the hills. That lasted twenty, twenty-five years, and when he returned to Nuoro, I came with him. To tell the truth, there has never been any trouble. Just one time, someone stole one of the hens, but it must have been Maria Conzu from next door. To tell the truth, Nuoro isn't a place where a robbery like that could happen, not with such violence. And times have changed. But bad men like that still exist and you have to be on your guard.'

But Marianna was not interested in these reflections. She pressed her little feet against the woman's hard stomach and insisted, raising her head from the pillow: 'How was it you became a boy? What made you become a boy? Did you snap branches over your knee? Did you pull nails out with your teeth? Come on, tell me! So you were a manservant, not a serving woman! Come on, tell me! "To tell the truth…"'

'Yes, to tell the truth, I would have preferred to be a manservant.'

Then Marianna's stifled laugh filled the mysterious gloom of the attic with joy.

And then the stories began again.

With the passing of so many years, Fidela's views on life had become entrenched. While Marianna lingered in the courtyard towards evening in the shadows of a pergola turned black against the darkening pink of the sky, there she was, nailing down a plank of the outer door which had warped and come loose in the heat of the June sun.

Marianna had given her the nails and then sat in the half-light, looking up from time to time at the new moon which was setting with the slow languor of an eye voluptuously half-closing. And in her own eyes, as she thought about her secret, there was something of the moon's softness. But the servant's presence irritated her. Day by day, hour by hour, the problem grew ever more urgent in her thoughts: What if Simone were to come?

How could she receive him? How could she escape the vigilance of the guardian of her prison?

There was still time, but she was constantly waiting, waiting, and in the silence she seemed to hear his footsteps approaching ever closer.

Her days had become a single spellbound dream of waiting. She waited just as anxiously for her father's return, for Sebastiano's visits, for the feast days when she could go to Mass and breathe the same air beside the sisters of Simone: everything was good provided it brought something of him to her.

When Fidela withdrew inside, having finished nailing the plank, Marianna rose and went over to the door, opening it cautiously, leaning out to look up and down the street. It was a Saturday evening, and perhaps their manservant, at least, would have come down from the Sierra. But the dusk thickened and even the swallows were retiring, drawing one last furrow across the reddening sky and over the black houses, and no one came. At the end of the empty street, above the reddish towers of the church, a single red cloud curved like an arch of fire. Everything was black and blood-red, everything burned with a mysterious flame which the darkness was gradually extinguishing. And a chorus of voices, young peasants singing their love songs, filled the air with nostalgic ardour. She leant her temple against the doorpost, thinking how her lover was unable to sing for her under her window. How far they were from each other! As far apart as the world's two poles; so far in fact, that one might even have doubted his existence... but now, as she thought more clearly, her heart swelled from its very sense of desperation: the sound of his footsteps rose inside her, and deep in her heart it was his voice she heard singing, filling the air with cries of love.

She drew back under the pergola, raising her head every time the sound of footsteps came to her ears from outside, for as long as Fidela remained indoors. But the servant returned to the courtyard and crossed it to close the outer door again.

'No, leave it open a little!' Marianna said sharply.

'Someone could come in.'

'If someone comes in, let them come in!'

Fidela resolutely closed it, not answering. The sound her heavy shoes made on the courtyard paving stones really did seem like a gaoler's.

'Let's get on, it's ready.'

She lit the oil lamp by holding its wick to the flame in the hearth and prepared the table. The meal was frugal, almost a poor family's meal: a loaf of bread baked with cheese and herbs; but a whole round of cheese stood on the table, and the servant kept cutting thick slices, eating quantities of bread with it like a shepherd. Then she lifted the water jug and drank deeply, while Marianna, as if annoyed by such coarse serenity, took only a piece of hard bread and went back outside.

The crickets were singing among the leaves of the vines and in the distance a horned owl uttered its sad cry. Where was Simone? In the mystery of the night, or the lament of the owl. Or in the approaching footsteps. The footsteps stopped outside the street door and she jumped to her feet, her heart thumping painfully. She crossed the courtyard, opened the door and could immediately smell the tang of tobacco and wooded countryside that told her it was Sebastiano.

'Aha!' he said, entering, with a touch of malice as ever in his voice and his glance. 'Expecting me, were you?'

They sat down outside the house door and he leant forward, calling to the servant.

'Hey, come here. I saw five men loitering at the corner of your alley, hooded and masked. God's my witness, they might be robbers. Watch out tonight, zia Fidè.'

'You can stay and defend us,' the servant said, not without sarcasm, 'with that little clasp knife of yours.'

'Zia Fidè!' he insisted, humorously threatening her. 'God's my witness, get back up in that lumber room tonight!'

Marianna laughed, but when he added: 'They won't touch Marianna, because they know that even if they made off with her chemise she wouldn't care a jot.'

'Why?' she said, becoming animated. 'Don't I care for my own belongings then?'

Sebastiano turned round, moved his stool closer to hers. He was in a joking mood this evening, but some of the things he said had bite in them too.

'The things you make, yes; but you don't seem to care about the best thing you've got, Marià. You let time slide by!

What are you doing all alone here like a weasel in its den?'

'What does it matter to you? Or do you have some proposal to make me?'

'I might have too! Meanwhile, ladies, give me something to drink! Give me something to drink, and good wine. Whatever else, you can give a man a drop of good wine.'

The servant went to fetch the wine.

'Have you been up in the Sierra?' Marianna asked, involuntarily lowering her voice. And suddenly his eyes seemed to glisten and she was almost afraid to hear his reply.

Yes, he had been up in the Sierra. He had seen her father, her manservant, her flocks, the men who were extracting the cork the Ozieri people were buying. And that was all. But simply hearing him speak of the places where she had left her heart sent a thrill through Marianna, a feeling of light in the darkness. And she waited for him to say more. But he was joking with the servant, holding his glass out for her to replenish, and tugging at her apron.

'Sit yourself down here, and pour, it's not as if it was your own blood. And tell me how you escaped, that time, in case your friends return.... so one of them was young and pretty, like a woman... what was he like then? And the hatchet, was it sharpened?'

Marianna began to find his insistence on recalling the dreadful event offensive. She withdrew into herself, while Fidela, who did not care for jokes on the subject, poured his wine without answering. Sebastiano put the glass on the paving stone beside him and continued: 'All the same, zia Fidè, one of these evenings when those friends are here, just you see if this Marianna doesn't settle down with one of them. Stay alert, zia Fidè, keep your eyes open… but you don't see or hear very well now; I'll make you a present of a dog, since yours doesn't bark any more, like all Canons' dogs. It's too fat and it sleeps all the time.'

Indeed, the old dog which the two women kept in the little garden never barked. Marianna, however, detected, or thought she could detect, too many spiteful allusions in Sebastiano's words. She began to grow irritated and said, in the frosty tones she could summon when someone needed to be put in his place,

'Sebastiano, don't be offensive.'

He picked up his glass and drank in silence. Then he answered, cold and stiff in his turn, a number of other questions she asked him, without attempting any more jokes.

They talked of pasturage and crops, of barley and lambs, and of how Marianna had wanted to invest the money from the cork: she wanted to acquire a holding adjoining her own but required further funds. She needed to wait another year or else sell some of her cattle, but it was a shame to sell any of the cattle, and all the more so given that zio Berte was against it because he loved his cows and his heifers. So they would either have to wait another year or they would need to persuade the owner of the holding to let it go in instalments. It was unlikely, however — it was out of the question, in fact — that the owner would be willing to accept instalments or wait another year. Perhaps he was already in negotiations with another buyer, perhaps there was a risk that Marianna might no longer be able to acquire the holding at all, and in addition end up with a troublesome neighbour. She spoke about it calmly, as if it was something that did not concern her. Nothing to do with farming matters touched her very closely, wrapped up as she was in those other thoughts. But suddenly Sebastiano became animated again. He turned his face to hers, staring hard at her through the darkness, and said, in a low voice that suggested they both understood the meaning of his words: 'Let's send Simone to see the owner of this farm-holding, to persuade him…'

Marianna shivered. She felt as if some monstrous black wing had brushed her, and for the first time she had a genuine sense of horror, of the distance that separated her — honest, conscientious, pure — from a bandit, a criminal such as Simone actually was.

Just for a second, diabolical new visions passed before her eyes: the street door flew open, Simone was coming, yes, as he had promised, but to assist her in committing some bad action, or even to commit one against herself, to rob her, to ravish her, to blackmail her…

A second later, and Sebastiano hadn't stirred, was laughing one of his foolish, mocking little laughs, as if pleased to have had his fun at her expense and terrified her. And she, in turn, reacted with violence, against herself more than against him. She felt that she had cast a shadow of doubt on her own soul, to have believed herself capable of the most monstrous things.

'Sebastiano,' she said, gravely, but with a tremor of anger rising in her throat, 'you get more foolish every day!'

For a long time after he had gone away and the servant had firmly bolted and barred the outer door and then seated herself in the corner of the yard under the window, waiting for the mistress to retire, Marianna remained where she was, silent, motionless.

She was still thinking about what Sebastiano had said; there was no longer any doubt that he was trying to provoke her; but she felt strong in the face of this behaviour: she only had to speak sharply to put him in his place. She was thinking, rather, of how she could escape the housekeeper's vigilance if Simone were to come.

It was difficult, as difficult as it was necessary.

Folded in on herself, while the light snoring of Fidela, who had fallen asleep, buzzed annoyingly in her ears like the scraping of a file, she imagined herself speaking with Simone, bent over her lap, telling her all his troubles and desires. And she was aware of everything, and listened to herself, and felt how she was made of two distinct Mariannas. There was the one who spoke to Simone, straining towards him like someone vainly trying to wet her parched lips at the water of a fountain. And then there was the other, a kind of overseer, coldly listening, ready to defend herself and to defend the incautious female. But when a man's footsteps echoed outside on the street, coming ever nearer, and stopped at the door, she felt her heart ache again. She jumped up, breathless, ran to open it. The man was a passer-by who had stopped by chance and immediately went on his way. She turned back inside, panting with distress. She saw the servant stiffen and sit up. But she felt it made no difference how closely she was watched; that, when the moment came, she would know how to overcome and defeat all obstacles. And she went to throw herself on her bed, exhausted, waiting still.

V

For some days Simone and Costantino did not move from their refuge, the former because he was waiting for the three outlaws to return — although he did not say so — and the latter because without his partner he did not know where to go. Costantino sensed, however, that Simone was somehow avoiding him. Even when they slept side by side he felt abandoned, alone, and was gnawed by jealousy. He did not understand the need to associate themselves with other bandits: they were fine as they were, just the two of them. Simone had once acquired a dog, one of those famous dogs from the Barbagia, watchful and ferocious, and had kept it constantly by his side. At night it had slept between him and his partner. Costantino had taken it badly; he had hated that dog the way one hates a man, so much so that when the animal became ill and died, Simone accused his companion of having poisoned it.

After that they had lived entirely on their own, partly because they were held in low esteem by the other outlaws. They lived on very little, with no great ambitions, concerned only with avoiding being ambushed by the *carabinieri*. Not that they were being hunted down in any case, because there was no price on their heads. This, privately, was a matter of some grief to Simone, as if he had suffered a wrong or an injustice. And if Costantino, who knew him well, wanted to humiliate him at times, he would compare the prices offered for the capture of other bandits.

'They're offering two thousand *scudi* for Corraine. For Pittanu, who's just a piece of dirt, a thousand *scudi*. Battista Mossa — huh! — a thousand lire. Even Bantine Fera is worth a hundred *scudi*. But he claims he'll be worth two thousand like Corraine if he does something really stupid.'

Simone would spit disdainfully, but he would feel humiliated.

The two of them lived off minor raids, and just once, at the beginning of their careers as bandits, they had attacked a dealer who traded in kid-goats, robbing him of his cash. But the deed had left them feeling ashamed, as if they had been petty street thieves; or else they talked of it as a boyish prank.

They imitated the serious outlaws only in seeking to earn the respect of the shepherds and cattle owners, to whom they offered, more or less tacitly, their protection against assorted malefactors and common thieves. When Simone needed a few hundred lire he went to one of these owners and asked him for a loan. And the owner obliged, with no expectation of being repaid. Or he would ask for a horse, or a heifer, or a ram, to buy, as he always said, but on condition he could pay later, when he had the money; and he never did have the money.

The shepherds, in any event, had no fear of them. They are more powerful people than outlaws, shepherds: they are almost their masters, since they are familiar with their comings and goings, their changing fortunes. Often they are their hosts and protectors. From their secure observation posts in the hills, they can easily fall on them, seize them and avenge themselves if they have been wronged by them in some way.

Costantino, for his part, received money from his mother. And the income from her pastures had tripled since he had taken to this way of life because the shepherds were so keen to have the leases on them. Neither he nor Simone liked to spill Christian blood, though they were ready to defend their liberty at all costs.

They lived through these days like hermits, feeding themselves on herbs and whatever they could catch. They spoke to each other a little, but there was an underlying hostility between them. Costantino, especially, was jealous at the thought of his partner's continuing preoccupation with Marianna, and his teasing smile changed almost to a sneer when they talked about her. Deep down, it seemed to him impossible that a woman such as Simone described could be so foolish as to love a bandit and promise to wait for him. If she had been a girl of fifteen, all well and good, at that age all women are flighty. But a woman of thirty, brought up as she had been, with so many likely suitors hovering round her! And he comforted himself with the hope that the whole thing was an illusion inspired by his companion's vanity.

Meanwhile the three outlaws did not return. Simone began to grow irritated, and often brooded, his eyes dark. The animal that lurked inside him was stirring. Then one day he was calm again, his face hard and resolute, the decision made.

Sitting outside the cave, while Costantino leafed through a manuscript of 'Sardinian Songs and Ballads', he was sewing up a tear in his sheepskin jacket and getting his partner to tell him exactly how to find the priest's distant farmhouse. He no longer muttered curses, as in the preceding days, no longer showed signs of anger or scorn for the absurd activity of his companion. The latter looked up, then quickly lowered his eyes again to his book, guessing Simone's secret thoughts. In the end, biting his lips, he said: 'Simone! The devil's tempting you! I'd sooner steal from my own house than from a priest's.'

Simone drove the needle viciously into the leather, bending low over the jacket, mentally working out the route without paying attention to him.

'Come on, Simone! For that woman!'

Marianna stood between them, she never left them alone for an instant. Simone went red; he raised his head and it seemed he was about to respond with violence. Quickly, though, he regained his composure and traced a number of lines on the leather with his needle as if marking out roads and footpaths.

In the night he was restless. Costantino heard him turning over, getting up, going outside and coming back in. He could not sleep either, but did not dare speak up again because in truth he was afraid of his partner when he saw him in that state. He could sense when he was not his usual self, no longer the good-natured Simone of their day-to-day life, but a man obsessed, a man possessed by the demon working inside him. At such times it was better to keep quiet, leave him to himself and his evil affliction. God would not abandon him.

And Costantino prayed, with his palm pressed to the relics that pricked against the skin of his chest like sackcloth. At dawn he heard his companion grow quiet and he too fell asleep. But he was soon woken by the distant dull rumble of a storm, unexpectedly blowing up and growing ever louder in the bleak early light. It was not yet raining, but from the mouth of the cave could be seen a low, livid sky; the air was close and sultry and the atmosphere smelled of sulphur. The thunder was breaking over their refuge with a continuous roar. It sounded as if giants were destroying the mountain by rolling its boulders down into the valley.

Simone rose from his sleeping mat and stood for a moment looking outside. The expression in his eyes reflected the weather, and temptation continued to churn inside him like the hurricane in the air.

Costantino, already sitting at the entrance to the cave with his book of songs, stared out towards the black background of the sky, where the east wind was furiously battering the treetops. But he occasionally turned his head and saw Simone carefully cleaning his gun, lacing his boots tightly and finally searching for something in a recess in the cave wall. He had to get to his feet to reach deeper, lunging forward in the manner of an angry cockerel. It was the crevice where they kept their reserves of ammunition.

'Simone,' he said, closing the book on his knee and leaning his elbow on it, 'are you really going out in this weather?'

Without removing his hand from the crevice, Simone turned round. His face wore a harsh expression; he cast a long, probing gaze at the scene outside, his scornful eyes as hard as metal. It was as if he were issuing a challenge to the storm. Then he resumed his search. He pulled out a cartridge belt which he fastened tightly round his waist, bending his head to see what he was doing; and when he had adjusted it to his satisfaction he polished it with the hem of his leather jacket and seemed to smile at the triple pouch that was attached to it, on which there flowered primitive roses, yellow and red, embroidered in silk. Lastly, he slung his gun over his shoulder, settled it comfortably, and stood four-square for a moment on the lip of the cave, looking again at the horizon and the dark glitter of water running down between the rocks and the wind-tossed bushes: he looked like a warrior about to depart for battle.

Costantino had turned pale; the eyes which followed his companion's every move were dark and unhappy.

'When are you coming back?' he asked quietly. 'To hell with you,' he repeated, anger breaking through. 'When are you coming back?'

Instead of answering the question, Simone gave him some instructions, as if to a servant being left to look after the house. Then he marched briskly away, but stopped again a little below the cave because large drops of rain were now beginning to fall with some violence, and streaks of fire, followed by fearful rumbles, flashed over the woods and seemed to fall into the pool, lighting its whole surface. After a moment's hesitation he shook himself as if the storm's rage had entered his body and filled his heart with a savage lust for battle. He wanted to defeat it all, he wanted to beat down the walls of the prison which had for too long held him in. Why should a few drops of rain and a rumble of thunder make him hover like a little old lady on her doorstep?

And he continued to descend through the scrub with long strides. The rain finally turned into a torrential downpour, driven by the crosswind into a veil stitched with blades of steel, twisting and howling as it swept in fury over the trees and bushes, which writhed with agony in their turn. On the open ground below, the ancient holm oaks, caught by this whirling net of water, shook like giant cobwebs. Jagged flashes of fire snaked across the heavens, monsters pursued by the wind; and even the rain seemed to be in flight, hurling itself this way and that, horrified by its own violence. Everything fled, driven by an access of terror; and all the things which could not free themselves from the earth's grip, the rocks glittering with dark reflections, the scrubby thickets and the madly waving grasses, everything that could not join the flight, contorted itself in desperate spasms.

Simone lengthened his stride still more. When he came to the clear ground he began to run as if instinctively driven to mingle with the elements. His gun and his leather jacket, drenched by the rain, gleamed in the greyness. In a very short time his cap felt heavy on his head and his hair was streaming water like the grass in the fields. And although his breath came in gasps, they felt like gasps of relief. He felt as he had felt that morning when he had plunged into the pool to bathe, when the name of Marianna had surged from his heart and burst like the thunder, filling the world with its roar.

When the thunder's din had eased, he became aware of footsteps behind him. He turned and stopped for an instant, annoyed, then continued walking. It was Costantino, following him like a faithful dog. He eventually caught him up and began to walk at his side, staring straight ahead, not speaking, his eyes seemingly fixed on some distant point. They did not say a word to each other, but carried on walking rapidly.

They walked side by side, in a rain which now became steady, dense, unremitting. Simone tossed his head to shake off the water filling his cap. He found Costantino's company an irritation, his presence more of an encumbrance than usual.

Towards the end of the day the rain stopped and the sun appeared through the clouds which had gathered in a circle on the horizon. Stretches of barley stubble glistened like pools of silver set in the green of the heathland. A young deer, its pale yellow hide gleaming with damp, as if the animal were made of gold, its alarmed eyes black as rock-crystal, crossed their path in a great bound. A woman on horseback, enveloped in a coarse woollen cloak, was coming slowly towards them, standing out against the fantastical cloudscape that formed a background. When she came up to the two men she glanced down at them, acknowledging their greetings with a nod of the head. She was young, and wore spurs on her feet like a man. Her large brown eyes, shaded by the hood of the cloak covering her head, resembled those of the young deer, but serene and trusting. And Simone thought of the woman seen by Marianna's serving man, and of Marianna herself, and said, shaking his head: 'If only that other woman was as brave!'

'When they're with us, women don't need to be brave!' Costantino retorted, annoyed.

Nevertheless he followed the horsewoman's figure with avid eyes. Simone laughed, but there was a certain tremor even in his laugh. And everything around them shivered a little as if the woman's passage disturbed the stillness of the countryside itself.

They were thinking that if they had been two simple travellers, they might perhaps have attacked her. But they were two bandits instead and they owed themselves, more than they owed the woman, a degree of respect. And against a breast roused with desire, Costantino felt the chafing of his relics and reflected that God sends temptations in order for us to overcome them.

This encounter seemed to bring them together, as if the unexpected shock had caused one of them to bump into the other's shoulder. Simone looked at his partner as if he had only then seen him.

'So you've come along too, my little gem! Do you know where we're going?'

Costantino did not answer. He bent to pick up a stone and threw it as far as he could; it fell in a puddle of water which shivered into pieces like shattered glass.

'Think about it,' Simone continued. 'I'm going to the priest's country house. The old woman might recognise you…'

'Let her recognise me. God knows us and recognises us too.'

Simone, irritated, made no reply. But the boldness with which he had set off was beginning to fade. Night was falling and the dusk was settling its own shadow over him. Yes, in truth he felt Costantino's presence could only be troublesome, like the risk of being seen by a witness. In addition to that, he had promised Marianna he would not do any more bad things, and it seemed to him that dragging his reluctant companion into this undertaking and exposing him too to the risk of being recognised, made his sin greater. From time to time, though, he shook himself all over to get rid of the dampness that penetrated him to the bone and to free himself also of his tedious scruples. And so they went along, he and his partner, both of them uneasy, climbing the path out of a valley; and it seemed as if they were walking aimlessly towards the clouds on the horizon.

At the turning of the path they saw a round cabin with a conical roof, against the background of the clouds, on the lip of the valley, with a fire burning at the entrance and beside it the dark figure of the shepherd. And they turned their footsteps towards it, for the chance to dry themselves off and get something to eat; but before they arrived Simone said morosely to his companion: 'Mind you don't give away where we're going. If you can't, it's better you don't come any further.'

Costantino came to a halt, biting the knuckle of his index finger. Then he looked up, his face hot with indignation.

'Simone! You don't really believe what you're thinking. I'm not Cain! If you tell me a third time to go away I really will go away, but, listen, you'll never see me again. Remember that we swore to be faithful to each other the night of the feast of Saint John. And whoever makes a sworn partnership before Saint John, as I have for you and you for me, that person is more than a wife, more than a lover, more than a brother, more even than a son. Only a father and a mother count for more. That is why I come with you, today, even against my conscience and at the risk of my life. And you treat me like a dog! The thought of that woman is eating away your brain, and for that reason I treat you with indulgence.'

Simone made no reply. He went on, his head bowed, to

see the shepherd, who was calling down a greeting from his cabin above.

They walked all the next day as well. By sundown they had arrived at the foot of a desolate mountain not far from the seashore. The mountain loomed black against the red sky like a pile of burnt-out charcoal. A little village of grey hovels which had been built into hollows in the dark rock like boulders in an abandoned quarry, its streets covered with yellow dust, added to the desolation of the landscape. Beyond it, the setting sun touched off brilliant reflections: down on the wild and barren spaces between the gilded yellow of the dunes and the blue of the sea, long streaks of marshy water, mirroring the sky, shimmered silver and red like giant fish wriggling on the sand.

There were sea eagles circling and calling among some jagged black rocks, perhaps left exposed by a receding sea. Simone thought one of these solitary crags would be a good place to stop for the night, as they dominated both sea and land. Leaning thoughtfully against the tip of the rock, he gazed out like a ship's pilot exploring the scene before him. Everything was quiet. In the shadow of the mountain a few lights from the village twinkled here and there, going out, coming on, like sparks in a fireplace damped down with ashes. From time to time a light puff of wind disturbed the scrubby vegetation and carried to them the smell of the sea. And the golden network of stars sank ever lower over the silent land.

Tired, but resigned once more to accepting Simone's orders, Costantino hoped they would spend the night up here, and had already huddled down, his arms around his knees to form a pillow, when his partner turned round, as hard and inflexible as a captain with his soldiers.

'Costantino, get up. You must find two long cloaks, one for you, one for me.'

And Costantino got up and went off without answering a word. Then Simone, seeing him disappear into the darkness, felt a sudden tenderness towards him, as if he were a younger brother setting off for some distant and unknown destination. And all at once he seemed to himself despicable, to be betraying him, to be doing him violence.

But these were the mere flickering lights of conscience, comparable to the streaks of brightness in the sky over the coastal mountains, not steady lamps. The hours passed, the sky separated from the sea and the eagles' sharp cries came again as they woke. What has happened to that imbecilic Costantino? By this time a quick-witted man might have gone and returned a dozen times over. Clearly he hasn't managed to steal a couple of cloaks; he isn't even any good at that.

And the sky turned pink and the sea appeared all speckled with drops of golden blood.

Costantino did not reappear and at first Simone was angry, then he began to be worried. When he saw the sun lift from the sea he decided to set off again, alone. After all, perhaps it was better that fate should have freed him from his companion. But here he was, returning at last, with a dark bundle under his arm, as unruffled as a servant who has been on an errand.

Simone unfolded the cloaks, shook them out, looked each of them over, judging their sizes. One of them fitted just right, big enough to cover his outer coat, and its hood falling to his nose.

'There's room in here for a church with all its saints and everything,' he said, while Costantino watched sadly and tried instead to smile. 'Try yours.'

'I already have.'

Simone took his cap off and shook that out too before folding it up tightly; and the birds rose and fluttered away from the scrubby bushes around them, glinting in the blue air.

They resumed their journey, following a path through the heathland that led down towards the sea.

'You can tell me now how you came by these, Costantì! You were a long time, but you did well.'

Costantino stared at the sea, and more than ever his prominent cheekbones lent his face an air of sad sarcasm.

'How did I come by them? I'll tell you. I bought them!'

'Now listen to me, Costantino. We're taking a big risk, and the profit may be small. Who knows? The farmhouse is up there; it looks as though everything's going to be quiet, but how can we be sure of it? If the old woman believed you, if she didn't take you for a half-witted tramp, she'll have taken precautions. She'll have hidden the cash and the valuable objects and she'll have called people to her house to keep an eye open and wait for the thieves. We must check first if the house is defended or not, and we must do the job in daylight. Trust me. I'll blindfold the old woman so she doesn't recognise you; and I swear on my mother's name I won't harm her. And now listen: you stay here; I'll go and have a look around up there.'

They had arrived at a strange, melancholy-looking part of the country. The sea had disappeared to the horizon and beyond the heathland, to the left towards the interior of the island, rose a chain of blackish hills looking like jagged teeth, but between the teeth the blue peaks of distant mountains were visible, suggesting a greener and more attractive landscape behind the dark barrier.

On this side everything was sad in the desolation of the heathland, which climbed steadily towards the brown foothills. On the heights could be seen a few small-holdings: small houses, grey or whitewashed, with enclosures of lentisk trees or prickly pears, silent and seemingly abandoned. One of these, between two shallow, rock-strewn valleys, standing on a mound reinforced by dry stone walls, white and proud like a miniature castle, was the priest's house.

So Simone moved forward, leaving Costantino concealed among the bushes in the little valley to the left. A narrow path trodden through the bright grasses of the stony incline guided his way. And all around the solitude was absolute, the atmosphere solemn beneath the melancholy noon sky.

He stopped below the wall of the mound. He experienced a sense almost of fear. He had the impression that inside the closed-up house someone was watching, ready to defend it. But he thought of Bantine Fera and pushed on.

Inside the small courtyard the grass was growing high, and golden flowers were appearing among the bluish foliage of the prickly pears. The sheep pen behind the house, the piles of dry branches, a lean-to like an old pile-dwelling, with its stone manger and the small forge for shoeing horses, it all had the feeling of some prehistoric dwelling abandoned since time immemorial. Was it possible that there could be treasures here? Everything is possible in this world, and in his present situation Simone understood it better than anyone. So he made two careful circuits of the house, gradually coming closer and taking care his footsteps, like a fox's, left no trace. The small windows at ground level, set high in the walls, were protected by iron bars — a good sign for treasure — and the little wooden balconies that seemed almost joined to the roof, the house door and the yard door, everything was closed. So he returned to the bottom of the little valley, displeased.

Their enterprise seemed to him too easy.

'Move yourself,' he said to Costantino, who was sitting waiting behind the low bushes and guarding the rolled-up cloaks like a treasure.

'A fine desperado's job this is! There aren't even any flies about.'

Costantino nevertheless untied the bundle and put on his cloak, pulling its hood over his eyes. Simone laughed, but wrapped himself in his own disguise as well, part in play, part seriously. And up they went, slowly and cautiously, under a hot sun that made them both sweat. The shadows they cast amused them.

'God help me, I look as if I'm going to a masked ball,' Simone said. But his light-heartedness was only a pretence.

When they reached the house they knocked, but no one answered, no one opened the door. Only a dog at the bottom of the valley opposite began to bark and other dogs responded. And the two companions exchanged glances with the impression that the dogs were mocking them. Strangest of all, when Simone leant firmly against the door, it gave way and opened. They found themselves in an entrance hall with the kitchen to the right and a small room to the left; and at the rear, a stone staircase lit by a small iron-barred window.

No one appeared. They went in and Simone called: 'Hallo there, is the owner about?'

Their only answer was silence.

The house was deserted, uninhabited. Even the furniture had been taken away. All that remained, in the kitchen, around the stone hearth where a pile of ashes lay white and extinct, were two old blackened stools, apparently waiting sturdily for the terrible event that had forced the owners to evacuate.

VI

The summer was long and hot; then, all of a sudden, at the end of October, the cold arrived. Mist veiled the already lengthening nights and Mount Orthobene appeared constantly wreathed in smoke, on the horizon behind Marianna's courtyard; the very rocks of which it was made seemed to melt into grey vapour. And the heart of Marianna too dissolved in sadness. Time passed: it passed fruitlessly.

Towards Christmas it snowed. On Christmas Eve, she went to lean at the window, and the village, the valleys and the mountains, turned to marble by the frozen snow and whiter still in the moonlight of a pallid sky, looked to her like a vast cemetery. She felt the grip of this silence even more tightly around her own house, of this lugubrious half-light, and it seemed the winter would never end. From time to time there came a brief dull thump as lumps of snow fell from the bars of the pergola.

The men did not return from the hills, not even for this special evening. In the afternoon Sebastiano had paid her one of his customary visits, affectionate but inconclusive, had joked with the housekeeper, telling her to lock her doors with special care that night since the Three Wise Men were already on their way and plenty of thieves were out looking for them, helping themselves to whatever else they might find while they were about it. And eventually, adjusting his cloak over his shoulders as he prepared to leave, he said to his cousin, looking her in the eye: 'Your lover is sure to bring you his Christmas offering tonight, a nice fat piglet. You can set some by for me.'

And so he continued to disturb her with his allusive remarks. Perhaps they were no more than jokes, but she always ended up with a wildly beating heart every time she saw him. And yet the name of Simone was never spoken between them.

When he had gone away, Fidela locked the street door. The evening's vigil promised only sadness to the two lonely women. It had always been that way, though, even in the Canon's time. It was his habit to go to Midnight Mass escorted by a manservant, not permitting the women to accompany him, nor to invite people back to the house; and when he returned he retired to his bedroom without supper, holding to his fast. No, it was true, Marianna had never enjoyed herself, even as a sixteen-year-old.

After dinner she sat beside the fire, and although bathed in the red glow from the hearth, she felt cold, she felt she was a little girl again, alone, secretly creeping downstairs to wait for her uncle to return from Mass in the hope that he might bring someone back and there might be just a little joy and celebration, as there was in all the other Christian households.

One year it had been Simone who accompanied the Canon. But on their return he had asked permission to go and take supper at his family's house, and that was the only variation Marianna could recall.

In any event, she did not care to recall the brief period when he had been her servant. He was another person entirely, the Simone of those days, humble and servile: one of the many melancholy images cancelled from the picture of the past, a figure drowned in the depths of a well.

When she had finished her tasks, Fidela bolted the house door and also sat by the fire, on the floor. Marianna looked up, contemplated for a moment the beaky profile of the servant thrown in silhouette on the wall behind her, and said with bitterness: 'What fun we're having on this festive evening, zia Fidè!'

'It's your own fault, Marià. You weren't born to have fun!'

'How ought I to go about it?' she asked, letting her head droop, more serious than the other thought. 'What about you? Did you ever have fun?'

'My destiny was not yours, Marianna! But certainly if I'd been in your place I wouldn't have had the life you have.'

'Tell me what you would have done!'

And as the servant hesitated to reply, she became irritated.

'You would have taken a husband, that's all, that's what you mean. Is that what's called fun? Yes, and tonight he would have brought his friends back to have a sing-song, and they'd have got drunk. And the only part we'd have had, after spending the whole of this holy day working, would have been to pour the wine, nothing else.'

'Marianna, it isn't like that! A considerate man, a good husband, is quite a different thing for his wife.'

'And where do I find this good husband? No one wants me.'

Then the servant looked at her warningly.

'Don't insult the Good Lord. It's you who don't want anyone. I am your servant and I shouldn't speak like this: but Christ is born tonight, and he said that we are all equal before him. So let me tell you one thing, Marianna. You have closed your heart as if it was a jewel case. And what's inside it? Only you know. But it's something that burdens you.'

Marianna had initially reacted with pride, looking up, eyebrows raised and arching lightly like the wings of a small bird. Then suddenly she did feel something very like a burden, a weight that was crushing and bruising her inside, and her secret rose in her throat and seemed to choke her. She bent her head again and a veil of hot tears pricked her eyes: tears of love, of humiliation, and of desperation too. Because now she had almost given up hope, was no longer expecting him, and her secret weighed on her soul like a dying man in the arms of someone who loves him and hopes to see him revive but is suffering the same death agonies. And the servant had read what was in her eyes, and thus she knew: the humiliation was greater still because it was futile.

Sometimes she felt she hated Simone. Why had he come into her life? He had taken away her peace, her self-worth, like sheep from a plundered pen, and had run back to the hills to hide.

Every Sunday morning she saw his sisters. They entered

the church in pairs, first two, then another two and lastly the eldest, as if to keep an eye on them as they knelt, perfectly motionless, on the flagstones of the still empty building. They were dressed in red and black, with those black bands binding their foreheads so that only the smallest part could be seen of their faces, little medallions of diaphanous pallor. They prayed, their hands modestly joined and pressed to their breast, with the rosary slowly circling through their fingers as if moving of its own accord. And the first two and the second two looked so like one another they seemed to be two pairs of twins. Marianna knelt beside the eldest and could easily have been taken for their sister. The desire to lean towards the girls and ask news of Simone made her heart beat, her whole person vibrate like a taut string. When they looked up at her in greeting, she seemed to be seeing his own eyes, shining from a distance, from the bottom of the well of dreams and pain. But she did not dare to ask after him and went away, outwardly calm, locked in her love that day by day was turning into pain.

No, if Simone had wanted to, he would have found a way and the courage to send her a message. A man who truly loves cannot live like that, as distant and silent as a dead person.

And a thousand worries gnawed away inside her. Dark visions, as monstrous in form as the clouds that ceaselessly rose from the mountain, swept through her mind. Then suddenly everything would be calm and serene again. The memory of his words breathed on her heart like a gust of joyous wind, like the morning star announcing a cloudless dawn of hope. The certainty that he would return would then make her lift her head and listen: and she seemed to hear the tread of his feet coming to her from afar, walking, walking through all the ways of the world just to be with her again.

Here he was! Even now, while the servant was grumbling on about something she was no longer paying any attention to, the sound of his footsteps came nearer. They were muffled by the snow, but she could still make them out quite clearly, quick, agile, sure-footed, like those of a mouflon on the mountain slopes.

The illusion was so powerful that she jumped up, leaning a hand against the wall to prevent herself from falling. Then she took a few steps towards the door, and as the servant was already on her way to open it and go out first, she darted after her and caught her by the arm, forcing her to stop.

'Zia Fidela, let me open it… and whoever it is, don't make a fuss. Zia Fidela, just this once, as a favour…'

Her pale face, her breathlessness and her pleading voice revealed better than any words who the person was, standing behind the outer door.

It made Fidela all the more anxious to prevail, since she sensed that the man her mistress was waiting for was an enemy.

'Marianna, be careful! We're two women all on our own, Marianna…'

For the first time in all those years of slavery Marianna rebelled. Her passion lending her a strength that was almost brutal, she dragged the housekeeper to the foot of the stairs, and there, in the silence and the gloom, her voice came out quite changed, harsh and authoritative: 'Go. I am the mistress.'

She never forgot the sound of the servant's heavy tread on the stairs and in the bedrooms overhead. Her footsteps had an oppressive power in the darkness, and it seemed that the whole house was shaking above her like a weight she was vainly trying to throw off.

She went back out into the courtyard, but did not open the door straightaway. She was almost frightened to do so. Someone was knocking at the street door, not loudly, but not timidly either. A low voice called twice: 'Marianna, Marianna?' and seemed to be rebuking her for her hesitation, for taking so long. Then in a flash both her long misery and the long winter disappeared: it was that night on the Sierra once more, with the moonlight and the nightingale's song. And it seemed as if the outer door opened by itself, thrown wide through some mysterious power which removed all obstacles separating the two lovers. Simone appeared, tall, dark, his hood topped with snow like a mountain peak. He strode in purposefully, as he might have done in former times, returning from the sheep folds or from Midnight Mass, and walked straight through to the kitchen. He glanced around, making sure they were alone, then removed his cloak and hung it near the fire as he used to do when he was a servant, slipped from his shoulder a damp and bulging bag, set it on the floor and stood up straight, his eyes sparkling with pleasure.

'Marianna! You see, I'm here!'

And shaking his head as if to shake the moisture out of his hair, but also as a way of saying: 'Yes, it's really me,' he reached out his two cold hands and held hers in them.

They looked at one another, in silence. Marianna was trembling, her legs ready to buckle. She felt as if his eyes were not just drinking in her soul, but swallowing it entirely, that their joined hands must never be parted again. And every atom of her will-power dissolved before him just as the snow he had brought in from outside was dissolving before the flames in the hearth.

Without letting go of her hands, Simone took a step back to see her better, then he glanced towards the doorway which led through to the hall and stairs and gave a soft laugh, making the same boyish gesture with his head.

'Zia Fidela would be right, tonight, if she said the bandits had got in!'

It was sufficient for Marianna to try to reassert herself.

'The mistress here is me, not her,' she said, her voice stern, trying to disengage her hands. 'Let go of me, Simone. Tell me what you've brought me instead. Let go of me,' she repeated, more sharply, twisting away because he was so close to her she was breathing in his own breath.

'You want to know what I've brought you? I'll show you,' he said at once, a little crestfallen. And kneeling down, he drew from the bag a package damp with blood. 'Don't imagine it's a stolen piglet, oh no! It's a young boar!'

Marianna stared down at it, grateful and touched. And she felt for a moment indulgent and tender too, as if receiving a present from a young boy, something small and simple but sincere.

Meanwhile he was unwrapping the blood-stained cloth from the parcel on the hearth stone. The little wild boar, with its red skin, its insides removed and the carcass stuffed with myrtle leaves, lay before her, its mouth open and its tusks protruding between its little white teeth. It looked as if it was trying, with its dying spasm, to make one last attempt to bite. Marianna picked up the cloth by the edges and put it on the table, then wiped the tips of her reddened fingers and sat beside the fire, signalling Simone to join her.

'Thank you,' she said, her voice calm again, her hands folded in her lap. 'Sit down, Simone. Have you been to see your mother?'

'Yes, I have. She's still unwell. My sisters didn't even want to let me in. Yes, I went there,' he added, now slightly timid and uncertain, reaching again to take one of her hands, which she tried not to give him, and rubbing between his thumb and index finger one of her fingers which still had blood on it.

They fell silent once more, not looking at each other. They were thinking the same thought and knew it. And it was Marianna who spoke up first; she let him keep her hand and asked quietly: 'Did you tell your mother you were coming here?'

'I told her, Marianna.'

'You did right, Simone. And what did she say?'

'She said I wasn't to cause you any harm. And know this, Marianna, I pay attention to my conscience. That's why I didn't come before now. Marianna, listen: by my faith as a Christian, I'm afraid of causing you harm, and even my partner warned me too and said the same. And yet… and yet I couldn't resist the desire to see you again… and you? Were you waiting for me?'

Marianna remained silent. She felt her heart swell and a lump constrict her throat. Reality had never seemed clearer to her than in that dream-like moment. She knew that her destiny and Simone's depended on a single word from her, and she would have wished not to utter it. Everything forbade her to say it, yet she could not lie.

'Yes, I was waiting for you.'

And promptly she withdrew her hand from his and sat

hunched over herself as if borne down by the weight of her responsibility. But he seemed to have become a different man: he sat up straight and began to look around him, with glittering eyes.

'You were waiting for me! Marianna, so I did right to come. And now?'

She could only respond with an ambiguous gesture.

'Now we are here… together.'

'Together…' he echoed. But for the third time they fell silent as if they were miles apart and had nothing more to say to one another.

"Together!" Simone was thinking, head lowered, humiliated by his powerlessness to act. "What's the point of being so close if I can't touch her? What have I come for?"

"Together," she was thinking, stiffening in her instinctive self-pride. "But it's no good my having waited for him all this time; it's no good his coming unless he loves me with the same love I feel for him." But not even she knew what that love was; there could only exist one kind of love between her and Simone, a love made of grief and the setting aside of all hope. She had waited months and months and he had walked miles and miles to get here. And yet all her waiting and all his walking were without purpose if mutual pride still divided them.

'What have you been doing all this time since we last saw each other?' she eventually asked.

Simone seemed to hesitate, to become wary. Then he smiled.

'What have I been doing? Well, I'll tell you. Hear me out.'

He related the adventure of the deserted farmhouse, and

how he had spent the rest of the time with his companion, nearly always hiding out in their mountain refuge like two hermits, living off the pickings from trivial raids, quarrelling over trivial things, singing and laughing together. In the end, towards autumn, Costantino had fallen ill. He had wanted to go up to the little church at the top of the mountain to pray; and he had thought he was being followed, hunted through the wooded slopes like a stag. So as not to give his companion away, he had not returned to the cave, but spent the night and the next day in a ditch in the bottom of the valley towards Olzai.

'And I saw him when he came back after three days: he had death in his face. He had a high fever and pneumonia and kept talking of running away. I made him lie down on warm skins, I lit fires all round him, I held tight to his hands, sitting next to him, for a week. I sweated with him, God help me, and was delirious with him. He still thought he was a fugitive being chased, and I fled at his side. Then when he was a little better I went to his mother and she came up with me and stayed with us for three days. That's what really helped him, cured him. Then someone else came up to us, one day this last November, yes it would be about five weeks ago, a man came up to see us, Bantine Fera...'

He pronounced the name in hushed tones, almost religiously, but also fearfully, and with a trace of vanity. And he quickly looked up to see the effect his words produced on Marianna. Marianna was listening quietly, her face in her hands. The name of Bantine Fera struck her as no more significant or terrible than that of Costantino Moro. The pair of them merely spread a little more darkness in the depths of her heart; and Simone felt offended.

'You know who Bantine Fera is! He's brave and ferocious too, if need be. But he loves me; yes, he loves me like a brother. So, as I said, he came up… it was the second time he'd been to look for me.'

He suddenly stopped talking. Since Marianna failed to appreciate the importance of Bantine Fera's journeying to their hideout, it was pointless telling her what ensued. But his words were also halted by an obscure instinct to be careful what he said. So he spoke of other, minor adventures; every now and again, however, the name of this new associate escaped his lips.

Marianna listened, still holding herself tightly in. When his stories ran out she glanced up and her expression was so sad and serious that Simone's face darkened.

'Are you displeased?'

Instead of answering, she asked: 'And what if the old woman had been there?'

'What old woman?'

'The one at the farmhouse.'

Every time he thought about that particular adventure, Simone experienced a rush of hilarity. He laughed therefore, and caught her hand again and pressed it to his chest.

'Perhaps you're jealous of the old woman at the farmhouse? If she'd been there, we'd have made her dance, that's all, I swear on my conscience. Marianna, I don't like the sight of blood. Marianna, didn't you notice how I wiped it off your finger? But you don't believe me, you're not pleased with me. And yet, look at me,' he said, turning to face her directly and making her sit up straight. 'Look at me in the face, look at me! Do I look like an evil man? Do I? And if you thought I was evil, would you love me? Would you?'

'No,' she replied at once.

'Well then, sit up and look at me. Don't be ashamed to look at me, Marianna! I can overcome anything, I'll win any war. But I'll also surrender and turn myself in, if necessary. Don't all wars produce prisoners? And then I'll be free and I'll come back and be your servant, I'll dig the earth at your feet so the stones don't hurt you. What more do you want from me? Just say it, what do you want from me? Tell me, Marianna. Yes, I don't deny it: before I met you again, prison and death and hell were all the same to me. All I wanted was to live out there among the rocks and scrub like the wild boar. What did any of the rest matter? Yes, and I was waiting for the right time, waiting for the chance to become rich and help my family. Nothing else mattered to me. But now everything has changed. When Costantino's mother came up to us, they prayed, mother and son, as if the cave had been a church. They said the litanies to the sound of the wind. And yet, Marianna, I swear, I was crouching out of the way at the back of the cave and my lips never moved but I was praying with them. This is what you've made me do: as God's my help, you've made me return to you like a little child. That's how I am, Marianna! Look at me!'

And she looked at him with eyes so wet with desire that he remembered the spring that tumbled into the pool in the woods around his refuge, and he seemed to plunge into it, to submerge entirely, to die there. He leaned his head on her breast and then let it slide to her lap, as if he had suddenly fallen asleep. And she in turn remembered their first encounter, the song of the nightingale that purified the night and seemed to drive away every spirit of evil around them. And she passed her hand over her eyes to drag away the veil of pride that kept her apart from him.

And look, yes, the veil fell, the wall fell. Now she saw him properly, the Simone for whom she had waited and waited, the Simone who had walked and walked to be with her. Here he was, his head in her lap, returning indeed like a child. He was the man with his head laid on the woman's knee, the innocent boy to whom the mother teaches the way of virtue.

Then she no longer felt shame, nor fear, nor pride: her only feeling was an almost frightening sense of responsibility. A man was there, at her feet: she could cut him down like a flower, use him like a weapon. A few words and his destiny could be set.

She hesitated, therefore, to say anything. She ran her fingers through his damp hair and her knees trembled slightly under the weight of his head.

'Get up,' she said in the end. 'You know what I want from you, Simone. Don't think I want it because I'm afraid. I want you to come back here as a true innocent, I want you to wash your soul clean the way you wash your face in the stream. I have waited six months for you and I will wait six years, twenty years, but you must come to me like a person newly baptised. Until you do you will be wandering in hopeless circles like Lucifer expelled from heaven and the devil will be your constant companion. And to keep you company and suck your blood, the devil will take the form of a man. It could be Costantino Moro, it could be Bantine Fera, it could be anyone, but it will be the devil. And at times he'll be so close to you that you'll think you're carrying him inside you.'

'It's true!' he said with a deep sigh.

'Well, Simone, you must give the devil the slip. You need to shut yourself away as if you've gone to stay in a monastery, as a punishment and as penance. But first you must fully examine your conscience, and follow my advice only if it matches exactly what you yourself wish.'

'Well, yes, if that's what you want,' he began. But already the cold breath of reality was seizing him with a chill more cruel than the snowstorm which had followed him down from the mountains. He saw again the faint smile on the wide, feral mouth of Bantine. He hesitated to make such a promise.

Painful seconds passed, during which they both felt, in the darkest crevice of their souls, the desire to have no connection at all with each other, to be quite separate, distant beings again, never even to have met. Marianna said, quite harshly: 'Simone, you mustn't promise anything if your conscience doesn't tell you you'll keep to it.'

He sighed again, a deep expulsion of air; it was as if he was struggling to breathe.

'Feel my heart, Marianna; to me it feels it's breaking. Yes, I'll hand myself in. It's what you want. But I want to be sure of you too. It doesn't matter to me whether I die or not, you only die once, but I want to be sure of you.'

'If I've given you my word and you don't believe it, what am I to do?'

They leaned together towards the fire, not speaking, as if trying to see their destiny in the shape of the flames. Again, they were both thinking the same thing but neither dared say it.

'I don't want to cause you any harm either,' Marianna said

eventually, very quietly. 'I have a conscience too, and now I don't know whether I'm helping you or harming you by saying the best thing would be to put yourself in the hands of the authorities. What if you regret it afterwards? Are you really sure you haven't done anything bad enough to get you a very long sentence?'

'Nothing that deserves a long sentence, no, if there's any justice. But I have enemies, and I'm accused of offences I didn't commit. I can swear, though, Marianna, I can swear on my mother, may I never see her again if I'm lying: I have never spilled Christian blood.'

After a moment's silence, Marianna continued: 'Don't think I don't understand the seriousness of what I'm asking, Simone. I do, Simone, I know. And I know what you're asking of me in exchange. And therefore we are equal, yes, we are therefore equal... Simone... yes...'

She flushed all over, turning red to her very finger-tips. Then she started to quiver.

'In which case, listen: there's only one thing to do. Let's get married.'

Simone sat up rigid, transfixed with joy. He caught her by the arms and turned her to face him. He tried to speak but couldn't; and he started to laugh, very quietly, on and on, like someone gone mad.

Marianna was scared. She stared at him, then mastered herself and found her voice.

'Don't laugh. Don't laugh like that!'

'I know... this is a serious thing... forgive me,' he said humbly.

Then he tried to think what else he could say to her to

121

please her, to make up for it. He could think of nothing. It seemed to him he had already promised everything, already given her everything. The idea flashed into his mind to cut his wrists and let his blood fall to the ground before her, because his sheer gratitude brought him a pain too deep to express.

In the end he stood up and pulled Marianna to her feet as well, gazing at her from head to toe as if measuring himself against her, meeting a challenge.

'Marianna,' he told her looking her straight in the eye, 'I'll be strong. You'll see, I'll be a different man.'

Then he gripped her round the waist, splaying his fingers to clasp her whole body between his hands, lifted her the way a thirsty man lifts a jug of water, and kissed her on the mouth.

VII

Lying in bed, Marianna experienced for the second time, as she had on the morning after her return from the Sierra, the illusion that the previous evening had been a dream. And yet, inside, her heart was fluttering as if it had grown wings and was longing to take flight.

The moonlight and the reflected pallor of the snow cast an eerie whiteness over her bedroom. A recognisable landscape was emerging outside, in the cold silence of pre-dawn; then the steady tolling of a bell fell in shards of crystal on the frozen snow of the rooftops. It was the early-morning Mass, and already Fidela could be heard moving about on the landing and staircase, getting ready to go out. Marianna listened to her footsteps with a certain apprehension: the fear of seeing her enter the bedroom, her chin jutting from the strings of her black bonnet, her austere and prominent eyes, silent and hostile. For by now her secret, like everything else she considered hers, lay in the hands of the servant.

She felt it would be better to share it fully, this secret, entrust her with the key to her soul; and then she thought that by flattering her with her confidences, she might secure her help at this difficult moment.

She got up, opened the door and called her softly. Then while Fidela came into the room, lamp in hand, already dressed for Mass in her severe costume, wearing her iron-shod shoes and with the rosary twined round her wrist, Marianna jumped back into bed and childishly pulled the sheet up to hide her face.

'Fidela... I have to tell you something. I received a man here, in the house, last night.'

And she quickly uncovered her face, revealing red-flushed cheeks and flashing eyes filled with an unaccustomed expression of pride.

'Put that light down,' she said, craning her head up on the pillow. 'I've something to tell you, Fidela. The man who came yesterday is my fiancé.'

The servant set the lamp down on the chest of drawers and turned towards the bed. She waited for the mistress to continue.

And the mistress continued: 'He is my fiancé.'

'He is my fiancé,' she repeated after a moment's silence. And she sat up fully in bed, frightened at what she must now explain, but determined not to keep it hidden. 'He is poor, he is younger than me, in fact he's someone I shall not be able to marry openly. Not that he has other ties on his side, but in the end we can't get married the way everyone else does. All the same, it's essential we do marry, for the salvation of our souls, and also because we have to save his life. And then it's essential, Fidela, because if we don't we could die in mortal sin. So listen to me carefully. I place my trust in you as I would in a man, Fidela. You will say nothing of this. Listen to me… we have decided to be married in secret. He has promised to find a priest willing to marry us in secret. I wanted to tell you this.'

The servant looked at her steadily and showed no sign of surprise. She merely wound the rosary more tightly, and slightly nervously, round her wrist.

'Who is this man?'

'He is a servant, or rather someone who used to be a servant, some years ago. I was a servant too, and that's how we met.'

'You? You were a servant, Marianna?'

'Yes. What was I if I wasn't a servant? And the man, you know him. It's Simone Sole.'

Fidela stepped back, horrified. The rosary trembled on her wrist.

'Marianna! Are you ill?'

Marianna sat bolt upright, her shoulders bare. She tugged the sheet up and held it to her chest, breathing heavily. She thrust her face forward in defiance.

'Yes, yes, Marianna has actually done this! You shut her away, this Marianna, you locked her up like money in a strong-box, and yet she's escaped. Yes, I'm going to marry a servant, an outlaw; what's it to you? Yes, and he, at least, doesn't care about the fact I'm wealthy. Yes, yes, I'm going to marry him. I am the mistress. I am the mistress of my own life.'

Fidela came forward again and laid a hand on her shoulder, her shadow seeming to fall protectively over the younger woman.

'Marianna,' she said, with unaccustomed gentleness, as if she really were talking to a sick person. 'You are the mistress, who's denying it? You can choose who you open and close the door to. It's not for me to pass judgement. But I ask you one thing: have you not considered your father?'

'My father no longer controls what I do. He controlled me from when I was a little girl, and he made me into what he wanted. Now that's all finished.'

'All the same, you have to tell him. Haven't you told me, and I'm only the servant?'

'No. I shan't tell anyone else, Fidela! I'm telling you because you are here and you see everything I do and I don't want you to judge me as something I'm not.'

'I don't judge you! You can send me away and do whatever you please.'

Marianna let her head fall back. A faint shudder passed through her. She saw the shadow of the servant fall on the bed, darkening the space where she lay, and felt a hard and powerful hand descend on her shoulder. And yes, it really did feel as if she were in the shadow of a tree or a boulder, sheltering from a sudden storm. She could feel the heat of Fidela's large masculine body and it brought back those nights as a child, the truckle bed in the attic, the fears and joys of living side by side with the servant.

Nothing had changed or moved on since that time. She seemed to be a little girl still. The same mystery of the attic was alive now, in her grown woman's room. The characters in the legends had come to life, the inexplicable things had taken shape. And yet everything was still a mystery. She grabbed with both hands at the arm held out to her shoulder, like a branch one clings to for support, and pressed her mouth against it to stifle a sob that rose in her throat.

'I don't know what's the matter,' she said then, recovering her self-control. 'I am happy with what I've done, but I'm scared. It seems I'm in a permanent dream and there's a hand leading me on. It leads me on, but I follow because it's what I want. I've thought about it all carefully, and I won't go back on it, not a step, even for my father's sake. It's my destiny, Fidela! It's no use your contradicting me, Fidela, and no use your speaking to me. This is my destiny.'

She lay back in the bed again and sighed as if relieved of a great weight.

'I haven't closed my eyes all night. Now I'm tired and I'm going to sleep,' she murmured, covering her face once more. 'I'm glad I told you everything. He'll be returning tonight.'

Fidela leaned over the pillow.

'Marianna, you are the mistress and you can do what you like, but since you've confided in me you must accept a piece of advice. Get your father to come home, and open your heart to him. We are all blind, Marianna, and we need each other for support. And then, you are a good Christian and you know the Lord's commandments. And your father is always your father.'

Through the sheet, Marianna felt Fidela's work-roughened hand lightly brush her face, making on it the sign of the cross, as it used to do when she was a little girl, to drive evil thoughts from her mind. She remembered the sense of terror she had felt that night in the hills, after that first look Simone had directed at her. But her thoughts did not change.

'Let me sleep. I'm tired and my head aches. I'll give you an answer later.'

The servant insisted: 'Give me permission to send for your father. Once that's done, you'll feel at peace.'

'Very well, send for him,' she said in the end, too weary to refuse.

Left alone at last, she experienced a sense of peace. Now that her secret was out, she felt freer and stronger. It seemed that it was there, lying beside her, her secret, resting on her heart, like a new-born son; and she fell asleep alongside it.

The servant, meanwhile, went to Mass.

She had turned the key twice in the outer door, with something of a bitter smile twisting her hard mouth. She would not have betrayed her mistress' secret for anything in the world, but she was thinking how she might save her. She had the impression Marianna was ill, obsessed: the obsession needed to be exorcised. If the Canon had still been alive, he could have expelled with his Book of Gospels the dreadful threat of excommunication threatening his house. But they were two women on their own, now, and she had little hope that Berte Sirca would be any help. He was not much of a man, Berte Sirca: leave him to deal with the practicalities of a shepherd's life, leave him with his heifers, with his curds and cheese-making, and he will do his duty punctiliously. But face him with another man, in one of life's crises, and he will fall like a leaf in the wind.

And yet it was essential to summon him. And to persuade him to leave his sheep pens, given the snowy weather and the consequent need to see to the animals, to feed them and prevent them dying from cold, it was essential to summon him as a matter of urgency. Having made up her mind on this point, Fidela listened to Mass with a calmer heart. She never turned to God to ask for help, especially in certain matters: God can help us in times of illness, and provide for our daily needs. But as for the disgrace we bring down on ourselves, as in the case of Marianna, God can also refuse to help us. Fidela remembered, besides, how she had in her terror invoked divine assistance that night up in the lumber-room of her unfortunate master and mistress. God had not heard, had not come to her aid. In exchange, then, he had endowed her with the strength to serve all her life without suffering too greatly over others' troubles and without having any further of her own. Her compensation was to be able to serve, to earn her bread and board and to help her masters. In truth, if she was now taking a hand in Marianna's business, it was because it seemed her duty as a servant. The grief and passion of her mistress did not move her; it was simply that she had to help the mistress. If the mistress had been ill, she would have sent for the doctor; in the same way, she sent for Berte Sirca.

When she returned, Marianna was still sleeping. She rose late that morning, Marianna, went to Mass herself, returned pale and sad and did not speak all day long. She avoided Fidela as though she felt too ashamed to be with her, and towards evening she sat beside the fire to wait for nightfall.

Returning from the courtyard, after firmly locking the street door, Fidela thought she caught a smile on her face. And she too smiled, a grim smile which flashed over her hard face like a flicker of moonlight on a granite boulder.

'There's no point in your locking up,' the mistress said,

mildly annoyed and with a trace of irony. 'You'll only have to unlock everything again, because he'll be coming back. He promised to come back and he will.'

The servant sat down without replying. For a few moments, in the warm and enclosed kitchen, the only sound to be heard was the soft thump of snow which continued to fall from the pergola. Meanwhile, the flickering flames in the hearth seemed to dance on the walls and reflect, in their changing patterns of light and dark, the unspoken restlessness of the two women.

Later, steps and voices could be heard in the distance, but they seemed to belong to another world, utterly detached from Marianna's.

'You see,' she said after a long silence, 'my father's not coming. You see? Even if I was ill he wouldn't come, it would be just the same. He values his animals more than me.'

'It's blood-ties that are at stake. After all, everything he has, they're all your possessions.'

'Yes, that's it, isn't it? Always about possessions, nothing but possessions! Why can't it be about what I told you?'

'And I have something to tell you too, Marianna, if you won't take offence. Do you believe that Simone, if you weren't rich…'

But the mistress turned on her with contemptuous pride and snapped, as if she would have liked to bite her: 'You can hold your tongue! What do you know about love?'

But Fidela was not easily cowed. All day long she had been turning the problem over in her mind, and like a bitter cud its taste still lay on the tongue.

'Let me speak,' she said, staring into the flames, whose

reflections made her pupils glow gold like a falcon's. 'Yes, I have no knowledge of love. For the simple reason that I am poor and I am a servant. If I had been rich, men would have gathered round me and would have taught me about love. Because it's the man who teaches the woman. The woman is like the firewood and the man is the one who lights the fire. In any case, what did you know of it yourself before this winter?'

'All right! But you can't say I didn't have men around me.'

'No, Marianna, you didn't. Who did you have? Your cousin Sebastiano, that passionate stick of ice!'

'And you, along with all my other guardians, why did you never let me get close to any of them?'

'Because the time wasn't right.'

'Ah, the right time. When was that going to be? When I was dead? Well, anyway, the time has now come. Leave me in peace.'

'Marianna!' the servant continued, refusing to be deflected. 'You seem to be afraid to talk about it. You seem to want to take revenge on something. But you're wrong, my poor flower. You're running straight towards disaster and you know it.'

'Yes, all right!' Marianna retorted, growing increasingly cross. 'I'm running towards disaster! That's what I like about it!'

'Marianna, Marianna! You're talking like a little child.'

'Whereas in fact I'm old, you mean! Yes, I know. That's what's wrong with me.'

'What's wrong with you is this,' the servant said, tapping her forehead with a finger. 'And then, you've lived too comfortable a life. You need to be poor and forced to work if you're going to deal with the realities of life.'

'And you've dealt with them well, have you? By doing what? Tramping round and round in circles like a donkey at the mill wheel. For the benefit of other people. Let me deal with them for my own benefit instead. So, yes, it pleases me to be doing this,' she repeated vehemently, sitting up straight and beating her hands on her knees for emphasis. 'I want to know disaster, yes! I'm fully aware of everything. My eyes are not blindfolded. I expect my family to be angry, I expect the whole town to talk. But that's nothing. Perhaps he'll be convicted and sentenced: that's my real anxiety. And this bitter bread is what I want: so that my soul and his soul may be saved for all eternity.'

'But tell me one thing, Marianna. Why marry him? Can't you convince him to give himself up anyway? If he loves you he'll do it.'

'Why? Very well, I'll tell you, even if you can't understand. Because I want to bind myself to him in death even more than in life.'

Her face had caught fire, her eyes blazed. But all at once Fidela heard her give a terrible, wild groan, and saw her collapse in on herself again with her face buried in her hands and her fingers wet with tears.

'It's useless to fight her,' she thought.

It was a frightening, unstoppable force that was carrying Marianna away. It was like the force that had laid waste to her old master and mistress' house one night: the force of destiny itself.

But suddenly Marianna recovered herself: she dried her

eyes and her fingers on the sleeve of her blouse and tossed her head back to rid her face of its tears.

'In any case, he has never done any real harm. He won't be convicted. And I'm marrying him because I want to help him. What is mine will be his, and the money will help to get him justice. And then, after winter the fine weather always returns. In a few months, in spring, this will all be over. We shall all be happy and peaceful. We shall go up to the Sierra to spend May there, and he will really be like the great tree outside the house, spreading his refreshing shade over everything. Why sit here now torturing ourselves? This is how things are. I'm not following the law of God, you tell me? God created neither rich people nor poor people, neither good nor bad. He simply said: "Love each other and bind to one another." And that is what we shall do. And you, now: get up and start preparing dinner for everyone. It's time. Be up and about it!'

The servant rose to her feet and began to sprinkle salt on the young boar, already placed on the spit.

But Simone still did not come, and Marianna fell once again into a state of uncertainty and anxiety. She walked out into the courtyard and stood by the street door, listening for any sounds. The silence seemed to thicken with the dusk. Simone had promised to return; she understood, though, how hard it was for him to guarantee to keep his word, even if he maintained the illusion that he was a free man. No, no one is free: she too now felt more tied and bound than ever, attached by an invisible chain. Why let it upset her? Better to huddle in one's corner like a slave and wait to discover what fate would bring.

She returned to the kitchen and resumed her seat by the fire. The servant was occasionally turning the boar on its spit.

It had been split down the middle and the outer skin was going black while the inside, under its dusting of salt, was turning golden red, with the inner organs dark and the ribs a dull white. The little teeth and tusks gleamed in the firelight.

Time passed.

The wine and bread were ready on the table, and Marianna, partly as a distraction from her anxiety and also to convince herself that the whole thing was not some fantasy of her dreams, went up to the attic to fetch some grapes.

With a cane in her hand, she stood looking up, choosing which bunch to hook down. They were all beautiful, every bunch. They hung in pairs from the central beam, as if from the pergola but without the vine stems or leaves. All the grapes were fresh and yellow, like little amber globes. She raised the cane, hooked a bunch, lowered it carefully and weighed it between her hands. It did not seem quite fine enough and she hooked another, but the cane snapped, the bunch fell on her and the grapes spilled down her body and rolled across the floor like beads from a broken necklace. She collected them as best she could, lifting her head from time to time to listen for noises in the street.

And before going downstairs again, she peered out at the little window. Through the glass she had a view of a section of the town, a vista of black and white roofs, and on the dark horizon under the lowering sky, the snow-covered mountain, stretched out like a giant polar bear sleeping through the night. The weather was changing: veils of mist were rising from the valleys and the air was turning humid.

The silence was intense. She opened the window, leant out a little and felt the frost press on her face like an icy mask.

The whole outside world resembled a great ship caught among icebergs; the sky itself was sinking ever lower, settling like a shroud over the whole sad scene.

And then, unexpectedly, a vision seemed to glow on the horizon, a shining sphere, as if the sun had suddenly appeared and the nightingale was singing. She hurriedly shut the window and went downstairs with the lamp in one hand and the basket of grapes in the other. And both of them, lamp and basket, trembled in her fingers, acting as counter-balances to keep her steady.

Simone had returned.

While the servant took her time fastening the street door, he strode ahead and met Marianna at the foot of the stairs. He bent forward over the basket and childishly took a grape between his lips and plucked it from the bunch.

'Marianna,' he said, a little disconcerted, gripping the hand that held the lamp, 'what does this mean? Fidela has just opened the door and let me walk in.'

'She knows everything. Don't be afraid of her.'

'Ah, that's not it!' he exclaimed, laughing. 'She's the one who looks afraid. Zia Fidela — here she is — well then? Is this how you guard your mistress' house? Opening the door to bandits? You did the same that other time too.'

The servant stared at him with her cold, clear eyes, her whole person communicating something hard and hostile, mistrustful, almost unnerving him. It was a hatred not for him personally but for all fearsome men of his sort and the dreadful things he stood for. A hatred and a resolute intention to do battle against him as if she were fighting, in his person, evil itself.

And looking again at Marianna, whose face had coloured on her servant's reappearance, he realised that the situation was completely different from the previous night. Between the two of them, reality had now raised its ugly head. The dream was over and there were matters that needed to be addressed.

He took off his cloak, but did not dare hang it beside the fireplace as the servant or the master does; he dropped it on a stool, like the visitor who must soon be on his way, and he felt a sudden sadness, a sense of unease. And even though Marianna, inviting him to sit opposite her, waited anxiously for him to speak, he was silent, head bowed, staring between his knees at the hearthstone. For a few moments there was a silence frostier than the weather outside. The servant turned the spit, then looked up, gazing first at Simone, then at Marianna.

'Well then, what have you to say, Simone?'

'I've come to rest awhile like the lonely wayfarer at the drinking fountain,' he replied, not without a trace of mockery.

Then he quickly glanced at Marianna in apology. Marianna smiled at him and asked in her turn: 'Well then, what have you to say to me? You can speak,' she added. 'Fidela knows everything.'

'Marianna,' he then said, 'things are more difficult than we thought. I've spoken with my mother, and she has been to a priest's house to invite him to marry us in secret. She didn't specifically mention your name. She just said that I wanted to marry a particular woman before I gave myself up. The priest refused, and said all the other priests in Nuoro will do the same. I'm frightened, like a hare caught out in the cold. My mother has not given up hope, though. Only… it will take time…'

Marianna had dropped her eyes and fallen silent, a little doubtfully. She seemed not to believe him entirely, and Simone's face grew hot.

'Marianna!'

'Well?'

'What do you say?'

'Simone,' she said, looking up. 'I believe you, yes, but I have a request to make. I want your mother to speak to me.'

'Fine. My mother will do anything you ask.'

Fidela turned the spit. And the two of them watched her, felt her presence in the room with them, inflexible reality. And she too had something to say: 'If you will allow me to speak, I will point out just one thing: marriage in the manner you are seeking is only valid at the point of death. And a marriage has to be legal. Why not do things the right way?'

Simone winked at Marianna as if to say: now I'll let her have it. And he shook his head, exclaiming with exaggerated gravity: 'But my dear zia Fidela, I cannot go before the mayor!'

'Yes you can. Simone! When the magistrate has released you. Why that bewildered look? What I say is in fact very simple. Examine your conscience and you'll see. If you're sent for trial instead, are you certain you won't receive a long sentence? If you are, all well and fine. And if you're not certain, why do you want to tie Marianna to you? What harm has Marianna ever done to you? If you've anything to complain about, it certainly isn't her. She is treating you as an equal, and you must show her that you are. Don't tie her to you, Simone. She is a woman on her own and has no one to protect her. At least allow her to keep her freedom, she can't be left to weep for a condemned man.'

'That's enough, stop!' Marianna protested. But a serious expression had formed on Simone's face.

'It's not enough, Marianna! If he loves you and you love him, then there isn't any tie that can be stronger. So, Simone, do you understand me?' Fidela said, standing up and placing a hand on his shoulder.

Simone was obliged to look up at her and there were both shadows and gleams of light in his eyes. And as Marianna was trying to brush the servant away, he reached out an arm and took her hand.

'Marianna,' he said sadly, 'maybe — it's possible — your servant is right! Nevertheless,' he added quickly, seeing her face darken, 'you are the mistress and you must decide.' There followed a heavy silence. Marianna withdrew her hand and did not reply. She seemed convinced of the truth of Fidela's proposition. Fidela, however, felt far from sure. She continued to prepare the dinner and did not speak again, for there was nothing she could add. But the mistress' silence and stillness again gave her the impression there was something solid and unseen which it was useless to oppose.

For his part, Simone was as miserable as the fiancé who sees his wedding day recede into the indeterminate future. He felt tired, his mind was in confusion, his thoughts dwelling on how he might at least have a few moments alone with Marianna to rescue her from the deep and wordless distress into which she seemed to have fallen.

When everything was ready on the table, the servant invited him to take his seat.

Marianna stood up too, and made a show of checking everything was as it should be on the table. She held up the bottle of wine.

'Fidela, for tonight's meal we need the Marreri wine: go and bring it.' And as the servant hesitated, she sent her a long stare of command with her dark eyes. And when Fidela left them alone, she took Simone's hands, pressed them together and bent over as if to deliver her words into the hollow between them: 'You are not a man to pay heed to the words of a servant. We must either marry each other or go our separate ways. You, I and your mother will seek out and we will find a priest who is willing to unite us. I will wait for you. Swear you will do what I want.'

Simone sighed deeply, relieved of a weight. He murmured: 'I swear,' and pressed her hands firmly between his own as if to seal the promise within them.

VIII

The day after Christmas, seeing the weather brighten, zio Berte thought he could leave the *tanca* and go down to Nuoro to see what the two women wanted him for. They had told him Marianna was well and that it was nothing to do with business matters. Why were they summoning him, then, if Marianna was well and other matters were running smoothly?

He set off all the same, but half-way was strongly tempted to turn back because the sky covered over again with thick cloud and it started to snow. Marianna was well, she was warm and comfortable, and all was peaceful in her well-maintained house. With the faithful companionship of the servant, she sat like a queen on her throne, whereas the poor heifers and the shivering veal calves needed food and attention. One thought drove him to continue his journey: he hoped that this might be about some marriage proposal for Marianna. Indeed, he kept asking himself who the suitor could be.

'Let's hope it's not a farmer.' However handsome, young and rich, the farmers he could think of who were available did not seem suitable persons for Marianna.

He preferred the idea of a more bourgeois type, a comfortably-off townsman, a lawyer maybe, even if not all that wealthy. Marianna was clever and refined and already had plenty to do managing her assets. If she married a rich sheep- or arable-farmer she would end up working twice as hard and risk damaging her health. A lawyer's business on the other hand earns him a straight net profit and he can spend it on his family without having to worry about other considerations.

And then, as things stood, he, the father, had become accustomed to acting as the master. To have another sheep-farmer or agricultural type in the family could only be a nuisance to him.

'But if that's what Marianna wants, let her marry even the farmer or the agricultural type. She's the real mistress, and she's wise enough to know where her interests lie. And time flies and the crop she's been cultivating for so many years must be ripe for harvest by now.'

With these thoughts running through his head, he finally arrived. Dusk was already falling and all was quiet around his daughter's house. He felt pride every time he entered the solid calm of the building which had once been the Canon's house and still preserved the silent aspect of a monastery. Inside lived his Marianna, his only daughter, like a carved saint in a gilded niche. Yes, and he, the father, felt proud and moved, because he felt that it was thanks to him and his paternal self-sacrifice, depriving himself of his only daughter, that he had created for her this position of wealth. And he took care to make as little noise as possible, entering the house, so as not to disturb all that settled peace. He dismounted, therefore, outside the locked street door and knocked lightly with the flat of his hand, whilst the pony, respectful, shook the snow from between its ears.

It was Marianna herself who opened the door, looking rather pale and troubled. Seeing her father she collected herself and stood aside to usher him in.

'Do you take in guests?' he asked, in a friendly, humorous tone, and yet respectful as well. 'Please to give a wayfarer shelter.' With his long coat, his snow-flecked beard, his rotund body and the little horse hung with bags, he did indeed resemble one of those figures in fables who emerge unexpectedly from the woods: no one knows where they're going, but they ask for hospitality to test people's goodness of heart and then reward them with much happiness and prosperity.

At the sound of his arrival, the servant had jumped up and gone to the kitchen door, lamp in hand. Zio Berte hurried over to greet her, thinking it more likely he would hear the good news from her lips than from Marianna's. But Fidela's face was hard, creased with dark furrows, and he had an instant intuition that something sad had happened.

'Fidela!' he said cheerfully, however, untying the bags. 'Why have you let this snow fall on your head?'

And he laughed because the woman instinctively put a hand to the white hair that protruded from her black bonnet. Then she smiled as well, her grim smile: after all, the presence of this simple and good-humoured man at least brought a little light into the house. He was not much of a protector, and it could hardly be hoped that he would resist in the face of Marianna's follies. But he was good, and goodness spreads a steady light over everything around it like a storm lantern that nothing can blow out.

Meanwhile Marianna returned to her seat beside the hearth. She was not afraid because her mind was firmly made up, but she had little hope that her father's return would help matters.

No, she was not afraid. Here he was, her father, sitting before the fire like the old man from the woods. His clothes were steaming, and enveloped in a faint cloud, he was glancing with pleasure at the wooden grid above the hearth on which stood a row of cheeses for smoking; and he glanced at the solid copper pans hanging on the walls, precious and useless, like the fate he had engineered for his daughter; and he glanced and smiled at Fidela, winking, as if to say: "If Marianna's suddenly been bitten by some new fancy, she can satisfy that as well!"

Fidela did not respond to his smile, however; and as the moments passed he felt ever more sure that some disaster had struck or was about to strike.

'Well, what is it then?' he asked, looking at Marianna. Then he added, to keep such gloomy ideas at bay: 'Anyway, Sebastiano came yesterday and I asked him: do you know what's going on at my house? They've sent for me to go and see them. And he answered me with a laugh and said: ah, perhaps it's about some matrimonial business!'

Marianna started. What did Sebastiano know? She shot a rapid look of suspicion in the servant's direction. And she felt an unprompted desire to make fun of them all.

'It's Fidela, as a matter of fact. She wants to consult you

143

because she wants to get married…'

'Marianna!' exclaimed the servant with grieving severity. 'How can you think of making a joke of this?'

'I have no reason to weep over it.'

There was something cruel in her smile; but her father was deceived, and seeing her suddenly cheerful like this, he thought that there really was no reason why his Marianna, wealthy and wise, endowed with so many good things and such virtue, should not be happy. Had she not, little by little, worked her way towards the gaining of this earthly paradise? And had not he, the father, separated himself from the most precious thing in his life, had he not sent her away from her own home in order that she might gain it?

'Let her have her joke, old woman! She hasn't seen bandits in her house, like you!'

Suddenly he felt an icy breath brush his shoulders as if a gust of wind had blown the door open. Sitting opposite him, Marianna had twitched her head back and turned deathly pale. It looked as if she had fainted. Almost at once, however, she straightened, her face closed and hard as marble.

'Father,' she said in a hollow voice, not looking at him, 'the person I have welcomed into this house and wish to marry is exactly that, a bandit. Yes, and to avoid prolonging this thing any more than necessary, I'll tell you straightaway who it is: it's Simone Sole.'

At first the man seemed to retreat humbly into himself, his hands clasped between his knees, accepting a *fait accompli*. But in fact it was the harshness of the blow that left him collapsed and breathless. Eventually he looked up in supplication, but did not meet his daughter's eyes.

'Marianna!' he stammered. 'A servant! A servant!' he repeated, finding his strength again. 'An outlaw! And not even a famous outlaw; it could at least have been Giovanni Corraine!'

'For me he's a bigger man than any of them,' Marianna said. And she huddled in her chair, face between her hands, determined not to have a fight.

The father, in contrast, stood up, working his shoulders to rid them of the weight that was crushing him. He looked around and everything had taken on a new appearance, everything was destroyed, as if a band of highwaymen really had swept through his daughter's house, bringing to it the desolation of death. Then he sought the faithful eyes of the servant and began to shake his head, his grieving expression asking for her help and advice. He could no longer count on Marianna: a dead woman sat there, slain by the bandits.

Fidela sent him an answering look and a nod of the head: yes, it was true; this was their disaster. But confronted by this Marianna, as pale and still as a corpse, they both sensed that any reaction of theirs, of grief or of protest, was futile. And this was the most terrible thing of all: the impossibility of fighting her.

Nevertheless, in his impotence, the man began to tremble. He felt bound and tied, yes, he felt defeated. But there were still powerful people, out there in the world, who could help him.

And he breathed a heavy sigh, almost sure he had found the remedy.

'Marianna, does your cousin Sebastiano approve of your idea?'

'My cousin Sebastiano? My cousin Sebastiano lives in his house and I live in mine.'

Her father began to tug at his beard with both hands, first one side then the other as he slowly shook his head. No. Marianna feared no one. It was useless to ask for help to break her will.

'But why have you done this, my daughter? Why have you done this?'

She did not reply. The reason why was something she did not know herself, even though she had tried many times to ask the same question during the long nights of waiting, in those twilights when she sank into the depths of her own conscience like a diver into the depths of the sea.

'What can have got into you, Marianna, my daughter? Simone Sole! A servant, a herdsman, a man who was never capable of making his own independent living, and not even good at being a bandit? Is he your sort of man, Simone? What is there about him that's bewitched you? What can he give you? Nothing! A beggar could give you more.'

'That's why I like him.'

'That's why you like him? But Marianna, are you sick in the head? You're not a child any more.'

'Exactly!'

'Perhaps you got on too well together when he was a servant here? You were younger then, and you were thrown together and no one was keeping an eye on the two of you.'

'That's not true,' Fidela protested. 'No, there was no relationship between them then.'

'That's right,' Marianna confirmed. 'But none of this matters. And there's no point in quarrelling, father. I've given you the news because it was my duty to do so. Don't try to argue against me or hurt me.'

'Hurt you! Can a father hurt his own daughter? Could I, Marianna, could I? It's you, you're hurting yourself: I've never done you anything but good. It was my true belief I'd put all my own interests aside for your benefit. I was wrong. Yes, I admit it before God, I was wrong.'

'Yes,' she said, moved by his humble grief. 'You were wrong.'

And he walked round to her side of the fireplace and stood there, like a servant, like a dog licking her hand.

'Marianna! Marianna, listen to me. Tell me at least that you'll think it over.'

She seemed to be lost in thought already, with her head between her hands, her shoulders hunched in anguish.

And they remained thus for several minutes, in silence, as if lost and waiting for a voice or a light that would tell them which way to turn.

'You'll think it over, Marianna, before committing such an act of madness. And then… and then, marriage! How can you marry him? And what does he intend to do, afterwards?'

'He will hand himself in to the examining magistrate; and if there's a case to answer and if he's convicted, he'll take his punishment.'

'As God's my help, I think I must be dreaming, daughter. I'm asleep and this is a dream. I'll pick a live ember out of the fire without burning myself, that'll prove I'm dreaming. But you're ill, Marianna. We need to call the doctor.'

She was quiet again, not responding to his words. Only when the servant thought to intervene, repeating the master's entreaty: 'You'll think it over at least, Marianna, before making up your mind,' did she raise her head and still without looking at anyone, say: 'I have already thought it over and made up my mind! Leave me in peace.'

Then she covered her face with her hands again and tried not even to hear what her father was saying. It was only the name of Sebastiano, uttered by him once more, that gave her some obscure agitation, a sense of foreboding she couldn't identify. But she was not afraid of anything. Even if Sebastiano knew her secret, what did it matter? What could Sebastiano do against her will and the will of Simone? No one could do anything against their combined will, if they remained firm in their love and their decision to do the right thing.

Her father's entreaties, advice and threats seemed to ring in empty air and fall to the ground like the pebbles that boys throw at trees to amuse themselves. And he understood his own powerlessness and eventually fell silent, defeated by her obstinate refusal to speak.

There followed more days of waiting and worrying.

Simone did not return, and it seemed to Marianna he must be lost in some unknown place, in the fog that shrouded the horizon.

The winter was particularly severe. At times the east wind blew away the snow caps from the peaks of Mount Orthobene and the sun made a playful appearance through the clouds, like a guest bringing presents and good cheer to a friend's house. But the harsh winter soon restored the mountains' snowy coverings, cast a shadowy gloom over everything and forced the land to sink again into its unhappy slumber.

Marianna felt as if she too were buried beneath the snow

and must remain taciturn, suspended in limbo, like the seed yet to germinate. And thus she spent her days, huddled by the side of the hearth, her hands clasped in front of her face. She appeared to be worshipping the fire. Sometimes distant sounds and cries penetrated the house; she remembered then that it was carnival season, but rather than signs of joy, those voices, those cries seemed to her to be the tragic howls of people suffering.

She too would have liked to howl, and could not. And yet, every morning, waking in her cold bedroom, its atmosphere bleached by the reflected light from the snow and the cloudy sky, she thought: 'Perhaps he will come today.' And at once the dismal day would open before her like the grimly rugged shell of an oyster and reveal inside a pearl of hope.

But the hours passed vainly and with the falling of night, just as winter cast its cloak of darkness on the land, so grief threw over her its black mantle.

One day, in February, cousin Sebastiano came to pay one of his customary, almost ceremonial, visits.

He entered the house with the rolling gait which Fidela had once remarked made him resemble a ship in choppy seas, and took a seat opposite Marianna. The window casements, wet through from the damp, had been thrown open and from the rusty bars of the iron grille there still gathered and fell fat, red-stained drops of water, like blood. An already spring-like air flowed through the house, the last icicles had almost disappeared from the eaves, and above the rooftops, bright little clouds appeared against a patch of blue sky, which seemed itself like a childlike source of wonder. Yes, the sun still existed; and in the silence of that quiet morning, the distant gurgling of water spoke of gentler times out there in the countryside: of growing grass, of dripping oaks shaking their branches like battered ships emerging from winter's tempests, of the new lambs in the sheep pens thrusting their greedy heads to suck their mothers' milk, of joyful dogs barking at the sight of a distant fire burning in the blue dusk of evening; and the fire they see is none other than the February moon slipping down between the almond trees of Oliena valley, the blossom already on them.

'It's the good weather that has brought you. You're a cheering sight to see,' Marianna said.

The cousin looked at her and smiled, showing his fine teeth against the pallor of his features. He was thinner and his complexion more yellow than usual, and the contrast between those healthy teeth and his ravaged face made him look as though he was just recovered from an illness. From time to time, even when he was smiling, his greenish eyes clouded over as if shadows were passing through the mind behind them.

A first glance was enough for Marianna to feel that there was something changed in him, something new. It felt as if their cool and rather meaningless family connection had been ruptured and that she was suddenly being confronted, through that veil, by a man like every other man, an enemy like all men.

'What a diabolical winter,' he remarked, rubbing his hand on the rough material of his gaiters. I haven't known anything like it for years. It's been like fighting a war. Every time we went out we came back drenched through. Ah,' he sighed, standing up, 'you have to be rich like you, or have nothing at all, not to have your head constantly filled with thoughts.'

150

'Yes! But we have had a lot to think about too!'

'You?' he said, a touch scornfully. But he quickly seemed to think better of it and turned his shrouded eyes away.

'Why do you say that?' she demanded, with rising irritation. 'Don't I have thoughts then?'

'You? Yes, you do. But it's nice to think them beside the fire, with everything comfortably arranged around you.'

'Quite right! And what about the things that happen beyond these four walls?'

'Ah, that's true. The damnable mortal sin: things beyond these four walls! The heart out of control like a ship in a storm!'

'Sebastiano! My heart is here, inside. Locked away as if it was in a strong-box.'

'Give me the key, then!'

'There is no key. The strong box has to be broken open. But what does it matter to you?'

'It does matter to me!' he asserted, raising his voice. And he suddenly shook his head and sent Marianna a menacing stare.

And she felt her heart, in its strong-box, beating nervously. And in the face of the obscure threat she felt a new emotion: she was frightened.

But the instinct to defend herself at once made her stiffen.

'Well then, what do you want?' she said, staring straight into the man's eyes. 'You have never given me any help, any love, nothing of yourself. And now you come here and attempt to take something of mine away from me?'

'Marianna!' he resumed, suppressing with difficulty the heavy breathing that rose in his chest, 'Marianna,' he repeated, lowering his voice to prevent the servant, just outside in the courtyard, from overhearing, 'I have come to talk to you about serious matters. Yes, the winter was long and hard and I didn't come, because I was struggling with my anger. It was like struggling against the gales. And then I believed it was all a joke, a passing thing.'

Marianna stared at him without blinking as if her eyes were the receptacles for his words.

'You are the one who takes everything as a joke. I, however, am not in the habit of joking.'

Sebastiano waited for her to continue. After a moment's silence, he asked: 'Is that all you were going to say, cousin? Yes, sometimes I make a joke of things, but this is a different situation altogether, it's turned serious. And so I say to you: what do you think you're doing? What about your family, your relatives: don't you want their advice? What do you think you're doing?'

He got up and closed the window. He leant against it and sent her a long look, his eyes sometimes bright with hope, sometimes dark with anger.

'Marianna, your father has been to see me several times recently. He's ill, and it's pure heartbreak. Yes, he seemed to want to confide in me but then he went away and didn't even answer my questions. So then I realised something serious was going on. Now I'm here: look at me, Marianna. I want you to look at me, I want you to tell me your intentions.'

She appeared to obey. She lifted her head and looked at him, but her gaze was mute, her eyes were limpid, as clear as a pool of still water that lets one see right to the bottom. She was no longer afraid. She had examined her conscience in depth and she had found all her true strength again.

'Sebastiano,' she said in her calm voice. 'You know that I am my own mistress. I love Simone and I shall marry him.'

Sebastiano pulled his cap from his head and beat it against his legs. He was panting with rage; he could not speak. Marianna had never seen a man so agitated. She felt sorry for him, but her pity was not without a trace of derision. She turned her face away so that he should not become even angrier seeing her so calm, and without meaning to, she smiled.

He was still beating his cap against his knees.

'Laugh, laugh then, woman! I'll say just one thing to you. None of your relations has ever asked anything of you, Marianna, not anything! Not even the most needy. It was like an understanding between us not to trouble you, not to cluster round you, to leave you free, free and peaceful like a flower among all the scrub. That's what you were for us, exactly that, a flower. You were the proudest and purest of our stock. Now, instead, you're dirtying yourself. And you're blackening all of us with the same stain. Yet in spite of that, listen: if your father is no good for anything, if he isn't capable of defending you and protecting you, I will defend you. Yes, I will, out of my Christian conscience: I will defend you against your own will, whatever it costs, even at the cost of life and liberty. Remember that!'

He clamped his cap on his head again and made as if to leave. Marianna jumped up and blocked his way, catching at the sleeves of his cloak, her face suddenly pale as if he had stabbed her in the heart.

'Sebastiano, you're not leaving! Sebastiano, what did you mean?'

'You understand well enough, I don't need to explain,' he

told her, trying to pull himself free from the grip of her nails dug deep into the cloth of his cloak.

'Then you must at least tell me why any of this matters to you. What does it matter to you? What has it got to do with you or with anyone else? If it's because of all these things I own, you can have them. Take it all, even the ashes from the fireplace. I don't want anything, I only want my freedom. But why can't I be free to do the thing I want to do? Family! Relations! Who has ever been concerned about me? None of you ever sought me out because none of you had any love for me. Only a bit of envy perhaps. And now you remember I'm here. Now? To take away the thing that you consider to be too much: my happiness. My father is no good for anything, you're right. He cast me out when I was a little girl because he didn't feel capable of giving his daughter a proper life. But he at least recognises his mistake.'

'His mistake?'

'Yes, he admits it. Here's Fidela: she can tell you how my father admits he was wrong. Fidela?'

Fidela had come up to the door and was listening. She was ready to defend the mistress if the cousin tried to attack her, but she contented herself with replying: 'Marianna, listen to the people who love you.' And she reached for one of her hands, trying to detach her from Sebastiano.

'Let go of me,' Marianna shouted, seized by a violent agitation. 'No one loves me. Who, tell me, who really cares for me? And if anyone had actually loved me, would I have thrown myself into the arms of a servant? It's desperation that's done it, because I was alone like a wild animal in the forest… I was alone… I was alone…' she repeated with a cry of anguish. And she pushed away the servant, released the man and returned to huddle in her fireside seat, sobbing.

Sebastiano seemed to calm down. He too pushed the servant away, signalling her to keep quiet and take herself off. And he bent over Marianna as if to listen more attentively to her weeping. Then he called her name gently.

'Marianna? Marianna, listen to me. If you were alone it was because you wanted to be, Marianna! You allowed your servant to shut you indoors as if everyone was a bandit. Who did not love you? I... I... didn't you believe that I perhaps loved you? Don't I love you, perhaps...? I know what has been happening inside me these last few months.'

And since she was crying loudly, his face turned ashen.

'But who could talk to you? You were a wall of ice, Marianna! You were like a queen, before whom even brothers feel mere subjects. That's how you were, my cousin!'

She heard nothing, so loud was her weeping.

Little by little he lowered himself to crouch at her side and remained for a while listening to her sobs. He seemed to hear the echo of his own misery; but he did not know what to do, what to say, to console her. And he even felt, deep down, a cruel pleasure in seeing her humiliated and defeated like this. It seemed to him that from now on they were equals, both of them impoverished, finally united in the true kinship of grief.

Without meaning to, without realising it, he timidly reached for one of her hands and touched its fingers one by one. Marianna shivered, stopped crying and raised her head, looking around as if waking from a bad dream. She did not pull her hand away: and now he spoke to her as Simone had spoken one night, in the same voice of a servant, almost in the same words.

'Marianna, listen to me. I have always loved you but I was afraid of you. I was poor, and you were rich. Yes, your father made a mistake. If he had kept you in his own house, poor but not an orphan, you would have grown up happier and I would not be crouching before you like an idiot. We would have loved one another; we would have taken one another. Today we would both of us be happy. But this instead… this… you may have thought I wanted you for what you owned. And I, well at that time I thought you too proud and I thought you wanted to marry a gentleman. That's why I was like an idiot before you… and now… now…'

Marianna withdrew her hand.

'Now… now…' he repeated.

He looked up at her in supplication, as if from the bottom of an abyss, waiting for help. But her eyes were clear, red as if she had been weeping blood, and as she gazed at him she shook her head and seemed to say: 'Now it's too late.'

Thus they remained for a moment, staring at each other, already distant again, thrust even further apart by the shame of having revealed themselves to each other in the starkness of their misery.

IX

There began for Marianna a new stage in her suffering. Simone did not return and a hundred different fears assailed her, now that her secret was no longer hers.

Sebastiano had left that morning with eyes full of despair. Her father sent her no news. Once again, it seemed that everyone had forgotten about her, shut away in her house as if within the walls of a prison. But those men of hers were weaving God knew what plots out there, on the pretext of defending her and saving her from herself. Then she jumped up from her fireside seat, prowled round the courtyard and opened the street door, peering through the gap as though to see what was happening in the outside world. She remembered Sebastiano's threats, and the silence and his absence increased her fears.

Nothing seemed so dreadful as this solitude of hers, this

powerlessness to make a move, to go against fate. She felt that she really was trussed and tied, unable to struggle; and she sat for hours on end with her cheek against her upturned palm, as if gnawing at the ropes that bound her, while every now and then her eyes, like those of a captured doe, scanned the space around her looking for a gap to escape through.

The sweet and misty breath of spring, permeating her whole body and coursing through her veins, only added to her restlessness. But the real grief that filled her heart, and which she tried to keep in check, was the same grief that had caused her to weep before Sebastiano.

Simone did not return…

One day, in Lent, she dressed in her best clothes. Beneath her scarlet coat peeped the pearly velvet of a bodice like the seed of a pomegranate through the split in its skin. Silver filigree buttons showed beyond the coat sleeves, trembling slightly, each with a pearl at its tip, its bluish tint seeming to reflect the blue of the March sky.

She told Fidela she was going to church. As she walked up the street from her house towards the cathedral she smoothed the folds of the material over her breast and adjusted the ends of the scarf under her chin. Finally she crossed her hands neatly before her waist: she thought they would already be up there, his five sisters, and she wanted to be their equal, like another sister, graceful and immaculate.

When she entered, the church was still almost empty, filled only by blue shadows towards the east and sunlight spreading across the nave in broad bands of gold. She went to kneel in the place where they usually gathered, and the gilded sphere over the altar of the sacrament reminded her of that night up on the Sierra and the way the nightingale's song had seemed to make the great oak tree shimmer.

The faithful were beginning to fill the church: young women, wives with infants pressed to their breast, widows whose tentative steps made barely a sound, old men with their heavy tread.

Every time the inner door opened a flash of red light spread through the bluish gloom of the nave. Gradually this redness seemed to flood the paved floor and warm the cold church like the glow of a fire. The women had all taken their places, seated on the paving stones, motionless in their duty of devotion. All of them wore their costumes of scarlet, with bands of saffron yellow encircling their faces like golden halos.

But the fairest of the fair, the five Sole girls, did not come, and Marianna, alone in her corner reserved for the afflicted or those in mourning, felt more than ever a sense of solitude, of exile from the community of the other women.

A new sorrow entered her heart. Not even they were coming. Why? She had left the house today to be among them, to feel, in their presence, that her love and her pain were not a dream. Yet not even they had come. Why?

Even after the sermon began, she remained stubbornly expectant. Whenever some latecomer entered, she swiftly glanced back at the door and lowered her eyes in renewed distress. And so she heard only a few fragments of the sermon, and the priest's voice, smooth and sonorous, seemed no more than a vague music floating high into the vault of the nave.

Only when the priest began to expound the parable of the Prodigal Son did she look up, concentrate and listen. He was young and handsome, the priest, with red lips and glittering blue eyes. His white hands grasping the edge of the pulpit, he leant this way and that like a man standing at the rim of a marble well. His fair hair seemed to reflect the shafts of gold falling on him from the Holy Spirit suspended over the pulpit in the form of a dove. The women were listening with more attention than usual; and indeed, they seemed to sense a mysterious breath of wind above their heads, a soft fluttering of doves. The older mothers who had errant sons wept with hope that they might repent, the young mothers with infants at the breast bent over them, fearfully raising the corner of the blanket that covered them as if it were a veil that revealed the future. Marianna was thinking that Simone too was a prodigal son who had gone out into the world to squander in evil ways the riches of his youth. He too would return. The words of the priest were a sign of that promise. But when the voice fell silent, the spell dissipated. The congregation began to leave. She remembered the objective that had driven her from the house and she resolved not to go back until she had had some news. She let the church empty. Weary, hunched in misery as if sitting before her fire at home, she had the impression that everything around her was uniformly drab: the very air was tinged with grey and over everything a chill was settling. Only a few elderly farm workers still lingered on the men's benches; and she rose to look more closely. Yes, Simone's father was there, decently dressed, but like a man in mourning. Long grey hair spilled raggedly towards his shoulders and his thin face looked hollow with grief and illness. His short white beard stood out against his sun-scorched face. He resembled the Prodigal Son's father as described by the priest.

Marianna moved to the altar steps and knelt again, waiting

for him to get up and leave. Then she followed him, quietly, treading softly, fearful that he too might melt away before her.

Instead, he walked slowly, sadly, gazing ahead into the distance with deep-set red eyes. Every now and then the purplish lips between the white whiskers contorted in an expression of disgust, as if he had bitten on something sour. And when Marianna caught him up and asked him quietly: 'Zio Franziscu, how are you?' he seemed not to recognise her.

He did not answer, but stared at her closely and his eyes suddenly cleared. She blushed: there they were, Simone's eyes, but far, far away, at the bottom of the well!

'Marianna! Is it you?' the old man said, stopping and leaning on his stick. 'My wife is not well.'

He continued to stare at her and his whole face changed, lighting up. And Marianna had the impression that she had had the same sudden effect on him, appearing at a moment of despair and bewilderment. And another thought gave her a secret surge of joy: if the mother is ill, Simone will come back to see her!

'What's wrong with your wife? Let's hope it won't be anything serious.'

'Let's hope!'

He began to walk on, the stick lightly tapping the ground. Marianna accompanied him.

They walked slowly, downhill beside the wall of the bishop's garden, then up along the stony side road, then further up a grass-covered lane. Finally, at the far side of a stretch of open ground from which one could see the whole lonely valley, already filled with shadows and the distant noise of the river, his house came into view — Simone's house. Marianna looked at the small building of grey stone with two little windows under dark cornices and an enclosed porch at the top of a flight of steps. Grass and nettles sprouted all round. She felt tears come to her eyes, so sad, so tragic was the face this little house presented to the world.

The women came out on to the raised porches of the neighbouring houses and stared at her, acknowledging her with a nod of the head. And she had the feeling that they "knew". It seemed her secret had spread and been picked up by everyone, like the scattered petals of a flower. But her own love gave her courage, and at that moment the only thing causing her to feel shame was the joy in her heart she was vainly attempting to suppress: the thought that if the mother was seriously ill, Simone would surely return to see her...

She raised her head and responded to the women's greeting. But she drew closer to the old man's side; it looked as if she was holding him up, as if she had found him collapsed on the ground, felled by some grave indisposition, and like a good Christian had brought him back to his own house. But as they approached the outer gate he quickened his step, his face pale and closed again. He pushed at the rusting metal with his stick and did not invite her in. She nevertheless persisted in the stubborn thought: I need to go in; perhaps I can bring a bit of light into this place which has been dark for such a long time. And she followed him across the small and empty courtyard and up the external staircase that led to the main floor. On the terrace, in a pot made of cork tied round with a reed, a blue flower stood trembling: and it seemed to her like a greeting. Unexpectedly, the old man, climbing ahead of her in silence, leaning on each step with his stick, called one of the daughters.

His harsh voice betrayed so much irritation that Marianna took fright and regretted having followed him in. She sensed that her visit was neither timely nor welcome. Indeed, she saw the large gold-flecked eyes of the youngest daughter, who had appeared on the terrace, stare at her with wonder and curiosity, then with sorrow and finally with a hostility that resembled hatred.

And while the father walked further along the terrace towards a second door, the girl seemed unwilling to allow Marianna to enter the small bedroom where the mother lay, groaning, in the throes of a fever. The visitor's face, however, was so gentle and concerned, even though her lips preserved their expression of pride, that the girl was disarmed. This was not the rich, arrogant woman who had bewitched Simone to make use of him as an awful kind of servant. She was not the woman who wanted to use him for her own ambitious ends, to serve her interests as a landowner and her desires as a lover. No, not this woman, who was anxiously climbing the stairs of the impoverished house and seemed to acknowledge the greeting of the little flowering plant nodding on the terrace. So Simone's sister stepped aside and let her enter. But when they saw her, the other sisters also rose in hostility, and they stood round the mother's bed as if to prevent Marianna from coming any closer.

But she advanced directly towards the bed and leant towards the sick woman's face.

'How are you feeling?' she asked softly.

She felt that only she and the mother of Simone could understand one another; and only their love for him could bring them together. Indeed, the woman stirred, turning towards her a face red with fever, the hair damp, though still thick and black. Her dilated pupils, swimming in eyes that were bright but troubled, stared into Marianna's and seemed to recognise her.

'Have you come back, Simone?' she murmured quietly, in a distant, confused voice. 'Your knapsack's just there if you want it…'

A shudder went through Marianna, shaking her from head to toe. She stood up straight and backed away. The mother had clearly seen the image of Simone in the depths of her eyes. And she had mistaken her for him.

Then she went to sit by the door with the air of someone who needed to justify herself for something, in the face of his sisters. They too had all sat down, self-possessed, their hands in their laps and were looking at her coldly like judges. She felt almost afraid of them and did not dare ask the question which had been her purpose in coming here. But she stared at the little flower, still trembling in its pot on the terrace, and she felt that the plant alone was the master of the house and was sending her some secret signal.

'Simone will return.'

And in spite of her pain and humiliation, this thought continued to reverberate inside her, sweet and profound like the organ in church.

Returning home, she found Fidela waiting for her at the street door.

'Here I am! Did you think I'd been waylaid and robbed?'

She seemed to be joking but her words had the cruel edge of her harsher moments. And since Fidela turned away, silent and hostile in her turn, she walked straight through the house, went up to her room and took off her church-going clothes. But she did not go down again even when she knew that dinner was ready. She leaned against the window frame, her face between her hands, and tried to assemble her thoughts.

Evening was falling, mild, soft, full of stars and the smell of new greenery. From up in the hills came the distant rushing of the torrent. All was silent and peaceful. But none of this could calm the turbulence inside her. The name of Simone had not been uttered by anyone, except the sick mother in her delirium. And yet she felt her visit had not been in vain. The silence and reserve of his sisters told her a great deal. Quite what she could not exactly say, but she felt they were sad things, and unfavourable to her.

'That's the reason he hasn't returned,' she thought. 'It's because his sisters don't want him to. They're the same sort as he is, the same flesh. They prefer to see him like this, they would prefer to see him dead rather than have him hand himself over to the law and to me.'

But deep down she realised this was just self-deception. No, if he wasn't coming back, there must be a stronger reason behind it. Only he could explain it to her; but he wasn't coming back.

She continued stubbornly to wait for him nevertheless. Perhaps this very night… and she tried to persuade herself, leaning on the windowsill, listening to the sighs and sounds of the night, the distant noises. Here come footsteps: the footsteps of the man whose tread rings in her heart… a moment later, and the heart refuses to deceive her: no, those footsteps are not his.

Then all was silence again. Smells drifted up from the

neighbouring kitchen gardens, from the damp beds of basil and flowering rosemary. From the squat little houses of the poor rose curls of smoke, indistinct cries of unfed babies. Around her, simple people with their everyday lives were settling down for the night, settling in their beds like a weary servant who has neither dreams nor sorrows. In some corner of her mind Marianna felt a touch of envy for those humble lives around her, a feeling of weariness with her vain dream.

She might at least have been able to defend her dream, save it from the dangers that threatened it: but not even she fully understood what those dangers were. She felt as if there was a wall in her way and her whole time was spent breaking her nails in a vain attempt to scale it and see beyond.

Suddenly she felt a blow, as if someone had struck her in the chest. She seemed to hear a hammering at the street door, as if to warn her that danger was real, that it was close at hand. Now there genuinely were footsteps, heavy, regular steps. They were steps she recognised, that she had anxiously listened to on other occasions, in some mysterious places. She straightened and pushed the window half shut, peeping through the gap. Two figures, two men from the town, were coming down the street from the direction of the church. They turned into the side alley. They stopped.

Not for an instant did her heart deceive her: they were two *carabinieri* in plain clothes and they had come to keep watch at the side of the property, where her kitchen garden was. They too were waiting for Simone to return.

For a long time she remained standing behind the window. She could see a star high in the sky and still hear the distant rush of the torrent. And she felt herself come back to life, become aware of things stirring around her, because now she understood the danger that threatened her and was able to fight it.

Fidela half opened the door and called her. Receiving no reply she crossed the bedroom with her heavy step and stood beside the window.

Beside the window Marianna stood motionless, her face pale in the gloom: a face illuminated from within by eyes that gleamed with brave determination, with hatred, with fear also. Eventually she closed the shutters and fastened them, and in the dark seized the servant by the arm.

'This is fine work, then,' she said sharply. 'You have betrayed me once again, all of you, from my father to my servant. But the deceit ends now. This is the end of it. Enough, understood?'

The woman pulled herself free.

'Marianna, I am sorry for you because you are suffering. But it is not my fault if your house is under observation like a house of thieves.'

Marianna gave a cry through her gritted teeth and seized her again, digging her nails into her sleeve as she had done with Sebastiano.

'Ah, you knew! You knew my house was being watched?'

'I knew: tonight isn't the first time...'

'Well you can get out! Pack your things and get out. And you can shut the door for good this time, because I won't be opening again for anyone, not even my father... not even my mother... if she were to return from the grave...'

Fidela did not answer. She ceased trying to pull free; on the contrary, in the dark she appeared to encourage her mistress to lean on her for support in the confusion of this painful moment. Marianna pushed her away, however, panting a little, repeating in an ever lower and more menacing voice: 'Get out. Get out.'

When she succeeded in driving her from the room she locked the door and returned to the window. She was trembling all over and her teeth chattered. She leant on the wall and gripped her head between her hands. Then she remembered the promise she had made to Simone: never to weep, neither in moments of danger nor in moments of sorrow. And she stood straight and stiff in the darkness, but without managing to still the convulsive tremors that ran through her body. Little by little she calmed down until eventually she gained a new composure, sad, aware. All was now revealed to her, as clear as day, and the light of reality illuminated everything. She was betrayed. She had started it by betraying herself, by revealing her secret. Why then should others not betray her too? And Simone would not be coming back because now, between them, stood the great wall of human malice.

X

In April she decided to spend some days at her farmhouse in the Sierra.

Once again, she felt worn out, as if exhausted by a long illness. At times, thinking of all that had happened, she still had the impression it had all been a dream. Then her pride, her love, and the regret and humiliation of having been deluded like a girl of fifteen made her start and blush.

She had apologised to her servant, begging her not to go, and had then wished otherwise: an intense longing for solitude drove her to shut herself away in her room for whole days at a time. She sought out the quietest corners of the house; or she wandered from one room to another, trying to escape from herself but never succeeding. She climbed up to the attic and after unhooking a bunch of grapes, sat on the servant's truckle bed. She felt thirsty but could not drink; she felt tired but could not sleep. The spring breeze, bringing the cuckoo's call and the smell of the growing crops, blew from one window to the other, rippling the spiders' webs in the corners and the loose reeds that had tied the bunches of grapes to the rafters. She constantly shivered. Her legs felt heavy, just as in the long ago days when she was a little girl and had been forced to wear new shoes with thick soles; and she felt the urge to be rid of them, to go barefoot, to be a child again. Then she smiled at herself, bitterly, mocking herself. Finally she bowed her head and became fascinated by watching her hands tip grapes like tumbling pearls from one shrunken palm to the other.

Christmas night remained stubbornly in her memory, Simone with his snow-topped hood. But it seemed a distant event, one of the stories Fidela might have told her in the nights of her girlhood. It seemed... all of it seemed distant, yet all of it was still there inside her, clear and firm. It seemed she had forgotten, and not forgotten a single moment. She felt she was no longer waiting, had given up expecting anything; and every footstep outside set her heart beating. She told herself that Simone was like all the other men, who made promises and failed to keep them. She told herself it was not worth suffering on his account. And she jumped up again, angry at being scorned, and prowled restlessly round the house, remembering his heroic plans, his offer, if necessary, to rip open his very chest to give her his heart.

Instead he was not coming back, out of fear.

But she wished to be a real woman, to live to heal herself from her sickness, to live to take control of herself once more.

She returned therefore to her farmhouse, to breathe some fresh new air and restore herself to health. Here she is again, then, seated once more beneath the great oak in the clearing: nothing has changed in the surroundings, and she too, as last year, is again a little bent and pale, a little older.

With nothing yet in flower, spring spread a uniform green over the farmstead, pure, austere, almost sacred. The level, shining grass of meadows so vast they seemed like lakes, from one outcrop of rocks to another, between one patch of forest and the next, rippled like water and reflected the blue of the sky, the shadows of the clouds.

And above the green and blue mountains of the horizon, the spring clouds continually rose like new shoots. They formed themselves into tight buds, they opened, they broke apart, they flew away like great rose petals torn off and bowled away by the wind.

A near absolute silence intensified the gentle harmonies of the countryside. And if a bull bellowed or the dogs barked, the echo wondrously transformed them into the voices of distant monsters. And everything around seemed to listen, amazed that any voices existed other than the light murmuring of the wind in the trees.

Marianna felt her whole being go slack in this silence, and in her memories. She had the impression she had never returned to her Nuoro prison; and this, for the moment, was enough.

Her father would glance at her in passing, or from a distance. He knew that Simone had not shown himself again and that everything seemed over. But it gave him no joy. He did not like the look on Marianna's face: there she sat, taciturn beneath the tree, while its shadows danced at her feet in the breeze and the earth sprang to new life around her, pale and sad in the midst of all her useless wealth. For her, spring has not returned; on the contrary, every shoot of life seems to have withered inside her. Zio Berte shakes his head, gazes in this direction and that, measuring with his eyes the vast extent of his daughter's possessions, then turns again to look at her, sitting thin and bent, like a reed, beneath the great oak. And life is short, and when you die you can take nothing with you, not even a blade of grass clutched in your fist, not even a pinch of earth.

But seeing Marianna's eyes turn slowly towards him, as if to tell him his pity is no use now, he retreats to the kitchen and sets about heating the stones for the curds. Partly using his calloused hands, partly using a large pair of iron tongs, he turned the stones over and over in the red-hot embers, cooking them like loaves made of bronze. And he spoke to them quietly, with a wink to entrust them with the secret.

'The thing is, the Lord has placed in our breasts a heart very like yours, hard, cold. But then comes a moment when it suddenly warms up, like you. And what if she doesn't want any other man? Yes, when man and woman are naked, as the Lord made them, what does the rest matter? We are all equal before God: and he turns us over and turns us over, as I'm doing now to you, my stones.'

He began by taking one and plunging it into the bucket where the milk waited, calm and white, with a few bubbles floating on the surface; and the milk seemed to wake up with a start and become a rolling froth; and so with each stone, until the whole bucketful was rolling and boiling, breaking down, turning to curds, turning yellow. Droplets leapt up, some falling as far as the kitten dozing beside the fire, who, feeling a spattering on his coat, merely flicked an ear. But one drop landed right inside his ear; then he stood up, arched his back and looked to see what was happening. Something very unusual must be going on, for the master had abandoned the pail of curd and had run to the door, tongs in hand, to look outside. The kitten seized his opportunity: leaping on to the rim of the bucket, he thrust his nose over the steaming milk; but as if he had seen a dog at the bottom of the bucket, he began to hiss and scrub at his nose with his little paw. He had scalded himself; he leapt back to the floor and ran to the master's side, but the master, even though he loved him dearly, pushed him away with his foot.

A man could be seen crossing the meadow, heading towards Marianna, a small man wearing hunter's clothes with a fur cap pulled down over his eyes. He was a stranger and zio Berte could not recall having seen him before. And yet he felt he recognised him, and it disturbed him.

Marianna was also looking at the man, who carved a silver furrow in the grass of the meadow as he advanced. And her eyes, after an initial start of surprise, shone with joy; then they steadied again with a glow which lit up her pale face like the warm light of a lantern. She pulled the edges of her scarf closer round her cheeks and forehead.

Her heart was beating fiercely; she seemed to be hearing the familiar footstep of Simone once more. How had she failed to hear it more often? She seemed to wake up suddenly, to have been asleep for months and months in a cold, dark place, in a cave, in a tangle of bad dreams. But while she was sleeping, Simone had never stopped walking, searching for her, and now the sound of his step was enough to break the spell.

Meanwhile the man had drawn close. He crossed the clearing and instead of going towards the house he walked straight up to her and greeted her with little bows of the head. He appeared to be smiling, but looking more closely, when he stood before her, Marianna saw that he was sad and serious.

'Hail Mary,' was his greeting, while the dogs under the tree barked insistently. 'You are Marianna Sirca?'

'I am.' She stood up. She was taller than he was and seemed to dominate him with her anxious gaze.

He returned her gaze; and before they had exchanged a word they seemed to understand each other as if they had known one another for years.

'Marianna, you know who sent me?'

'I know.'

'You recognise me then?'

'How could I not recognise you? And did you not recognise me?'

'Of course! Well, can I talk to you?'

'Do you have good news to tell me?'

'If you have not changed your mind, the news is good.'

'Thank God!' she said. And she turned her head as if taking in her surroundings and a sigh escaped her. She felt as if she had emerged from a hole in the ground and suddenly the space had opened up all round her.

But her father had moved from the doorway and was cautiously, almost timidly, coming towards them.

She went to meet him, and introduced the unexpected visitor: 'This is Simone's companion; it's Costantino Moro.'

'You are most welcome,' her father said in greeting; and she was struck by his benevolent tone.

They entered the kitchen. Costantino sat down beside the fire, after leaning his gun against the wall. But when the kitten began to sharpen its claws on the wood of the stock he got up and hung the weapon on the peg beside the window. He seemed to know the place as if he had been there before, so well had Simone described it. Yes, it was more like the sort of house one would find in town, not a mean hovel of impoverished shepherds in constant battle against men and the elements: a real house where everything breathed well-being, peace, safety. At the entrance were double doors, in the windows was glass, and the fireplace had the fittings of rich owners' kitchens, with its wooden grid suspended over the fire for smoking cheeses.

It must have been a fine thing in the winter evenings to stretch out on the sleeping mats before the log fire and listen to the voices of the forest in conversation with the wind.

He removed his cap, put it on again and sighed. He remembered his own house, kept in good repair, and his mother all alone, down there, grieving amongst all those similar good things; and it seemed to him that zio Berte's eyes resembled hers. Marianna had taken a seat opposite him, composed but with her pale face thrust forward in suppressed anxiety. He did not know, however, how to relay his message; he felt that zio Berte's presence made them strangers and enemies again.

Marianna said: 'Father, sit down.'

Zio Berte obeyed. He sat on the ground and asked Costantino, with a little wink to show that he could speak freely: 'And how do you come to be in these parts?'

'I've come from Nuoro. I've got a week's safe-conduct pass because I was serving as a witness in a court case

175

involving people from my village. Well, I came to look for you in Nuoro but your servant told me you were here.'

'You came to look for me in Nuoro?'

'Well, in truth…' Costantino said, embarrassed, 'I was looking for Marianna.'

'Yes,' she added, turning a trifle impatiently to her father, 'Simone sent him.'

A shadow passed over Costantino's face. If Marianna was talking like this, it must mean the two of them understood each other; and he had been hoping until that moment that a substantial element of self-deception and fantasy lay behind his partner's erratic behaviour.

'Yes… so…' he began again, then fell silent and lowered his head as if trying to order his thoughts. Eventually he turned to look at Marianna, asking her with his eyes if he could speak freely. He saw at once that her face had darkened as well. 'So,' he resumed, summoning his courage and trying to choose his words carefully before uttering them, 'you know who I am. It's clear that he has talked to you about me! Yes, we have been like brothers, for three years… because a man, you see, however wild he may be, always needs companionship. If he doesn't have anyone else he makes do with a dog… and this last autumn, I was ill. If he, Simone, hadn't helped me, there wouldn't even have been any of my bones left to find and bury. But that's not the point…' he continued, becoming ever more serious and at the same time more ill at ease, feeling that all this preamble of his did not deceive his listeners. 'The point is, man must help man. And so I, in turn, in my small way, when Simone tells me certain things, I speak to him with my heart open, and if he's wrong I tell him plainly. And sometimes he tells me stories that really seem to be just making fun of his listener...'

There followed a moment of painful silence. He continued to stare at the floor and Marianna, very pale, struggled to keep in check her turbulent emotions.

'Costantino,' she said in the end, 'you can pass on what he instructed you to tell me. My father is fully informed of everything.'

'Well, this is how things stand. He said to me: "I'm engaged; I'm to be married!" And I imagined he was just making fun of me. But then I saw he was constantly lost in his thoughts and I began to believe him. At Christmas he went hunting and brought back a young wild boar, and he said: "I'm taking it to her, to the woman, as a present for the feast." And so he came to Nuoro. When he returned he told me: "Costantino, we really are going to get married. Then I'm going to give myself up and take whatever punishment I have to take." You know the story up to there. Now I'll tell you the rest. He said: "I need to find a priest who will marry us, because the ones in Nuoro don't want to have anything to do with it." And so we went to another priest, it doesn't matter who it was. It seemed as if he was going for a joke, but from time to time Simone's face went as dark and gloomy as a dying man's. That was last January. There was a heavy snowfall. Walking across the flat lands at night, it looked as if we were out at sea. We didn't know which direction we should be heading. By God's grace, we arrived. The priest received us kindly, may God reward him. Even when he knew our way of life he received us kindly. But when he knew what we wanted, he started to laugh. "At Easter, at Easter," he said, making a joke of it. "And if the

177

bride-to-be invites me then, I'll go to her sheep folds and I'll do whatever you want up there. I'm sure you don't want to make me do anything by force." He was a cheerful sort of priest, as you can tell. When Simone insisted, he said: "If you're in a hurry to tie the knot, you can always cut a reed and tie yourself to the lady with that." But after a lot of arguing to and fro he promised to come here in spring, to marry you. And that was the understanding. And Simone set off to your house, Marianna, to let you know about all this. But before he got to the edge of town he met one of his sisters, dressed as a man, waiting for him to warn him your house was surrounded by spies. Do you understand, Marianna? Simone's sisters were taking turns to wait for him, dressed as men, at the spot they knew he'd have to pass to arrive home. They're brave girls. He turned back, waiting for better times. And he didn't even go to see his sick mother, and he didn't send you a message about any of this because he didn't want to frighten you…'

Marianna smiled. Her eyes gleamed with fierce pride.

'It's not for him to assume I would be frightened.'

'Let me finish. Day by day, he hoped to come to you, and he was reluctant to send you his greetings through his sisters because he couldn't be sure even of them. Then, when this good opportunity came up with me coming for the court case, it was decided that I should be the one to bring you his greetings.'

'Thank you. Did you put yourself out just for this? But here… here…' she went on; and she did not finish because Costantino said, lowering his voice: 'Your farm is surrounded by spies as well.'

Marianna started and looked at her father. Then she began

178

to smile again, sarcastically.

'Father, we need to show we're brave people up here as well. Very well, go and see straightaway where the spies are hiding. Off you go, quick, and tell them they're wasting their time.'

The father stared, and it seemed to him his daughter must be going a little mad. He couldn't quite understand, but he had the impression she was sending him outside so that she could talk more easily with Costantino; and without opening his mouth he stood up and went out, while the bandit followed him with eyebrows raised in a frown, offended.

'Why did you send him away, Marianna? He could have heard the rest of what I have to say; he should have.'

'Wait; he'll be back soon, you'll see. In the meantime there's something I have to tell you, without my father hearing. He must not be held responsible for what I say! Well then, there's no point in your continuing. I understand everything perfectly clearly. Simone no longer wishes to have anything to do with me. He regrets it now, he's ashamed of it. Why? Who has got at him and changed him? I don't want to know. Except that you can take a message back to him from me, just a single word. I request you to tell him, from me, that he is a coward.'

Costantino put a hand to his head, as if something had struck him. He reddened, then turned pale and dropped his gaze, leaning his head a little to the left in his habitual gesture of resignation. His heart, however, was dancing with indignation. If Marianna had been a man and had struck him, it would not have caused him such offence as this did, one lone and despairing woman. Part of him, however, agreed with her, and in trying to placate her he felt he was also appeasing his own conscience.

'Marianna,' he began; then remained momentarily silent, uncertain; how could he explain everything properly? How could he properly explain how it had been, in such a way that she — now thoroughly disaffected — would believe him? He needed to describe to her Simone's frenzied restlessness in those early days, his bursts of anger, followed by periods of tenderness when the two companions hidden away in their refuge, surrounded by the fury of the wind or the calm desolation of the snow, passed the time in singing competitions, improvising songs in whose primitive verses the figure of her, Marianna, constantly appeared, bright and far off like the moon darting between the banks of winter clouds? And how was he to explain the rest? The change in Simone, the anxiety in which he lived?

'Many times, many, many times, he set off to come to you. But he turned back in order not to put you in a position of danger. And in his rage he slashed and stabbed at tree trunks with his knife, muttering curses against everything and everyone. Then he would calm down and say: anyway, she's sure of me and will wait for me, even if it takes a thousand years... Marianna, what have you done to the man he used to be? You've reduced him to a boy again. He even said your name in his sleep; and he still says it, he's still like a boy. Search your conscience, Marianna: pay attention to what I'm saying. You must follow your life and he his. Don't you understand that he will be sent to prison? And he doesn't want to tie his fate to yours. But he does want you to forgive him.'

He spoke in a low voice, and even though he felt the spell that had bound Simone to Marianna was finally broken, a bitter vein of jealousy still seeped into his words of peace. When he said "he does want you to forgive him," he leaned towards her as if asking forgiveness for himself as well. But she sensed that he was concealing some part of the truth from her. And she had gone rigid and implacable again.

'Marianna! I have to go. Don't force me to leave like this, like an enemy. What am I to tell him?'

'I have only one word. I gave my word to him once, and now I have said one to you.'

'And I won't take that back as your message! I want to speak with your father. He's coming back now.'

'You will say nothing to my father, if you're a man! You came to speak with me, not him.'

So then Costantino stood up and made as if to unhook his gun.

Zio Berte was coming back towards the house after having been down to the spring in the thicket of trees at the far side of the meadow. He had felt the need to consult the things around him, the spring, the plants, the bushes, the solitude that was a friend to his simple soul. And he had put his hands to the trunks of the cork oaks to ask their advice as if each was a learned individual. He talked aloud.

'It's possible there are spies. Everything is possible. What I don't understand is Marianna's bad temper. Or rather, yes, I understand it well enough. How could she not feel bad-tempered, in her position? What an evil spell she's under! She distrusts everyone, she even distrusts me: that's why she sent me away... Ah!' he sighed. And God's name came to his lips but he did not utter it.

He had never been a very religious man. Whole years

had gone by without his ever setting foot in a church. And he was not even superstitious, even though simple-hearted. And although far from men and the affairs of the world, he nevertheless felt attached to these men and these things, just as the leaf at the top of the tree is attached to the most hidden root of the same tree. He was aware, however, of having sent his only daughter away from her home — out of vanity; out of love, even if indirectly, for worldly gain. And he sensed that he needed to atone to the full for his error.

And he went to drink at the spring, even though he was not thirsty. He knelt down, he saw his reflection in the clear, brown water, as if he were looking into a great eye whose pupil was the first gleaming of the moon.

'Berte Sirca, Berte Sirca,' he said to his reflection, 'do what your conscience tells you to do. Help your daughter.'

He returned slowly and thoughtfully to the house. He saw Costantino getting ready to leave. He had already lifted his gun from the peg and was pulling his cap over his eyes.

'You mustn't go,' he said. 'You mustn't do us that injury. Marianna will light the fire now and prepare dinner. Come and see her property.'

Costantino hesitated for a moment, then hung the gun up again and followed his host to the edge of the clearing. From there, the manservant could be seen, tall and calm, driving the cows home across the meadow, slow and satiated, their coats turning silver in the reflected moonlight.

Yes, Marianna was beautiful, proud and rich: Simone might well sacrifice even his liberty and spend years and years in prison for her. Costantino watched, and seemed to be himself under the sway of an enchantment now. Not only did he no longer feel his companion was wrong, but he felt a confused desire that everything could somehow be arranged. And he yielded to zio Berte's invitation with the hope that zio Berte might be the one who could speak the word of peace.

Zio Berte, in fact, was lingering at the edge of the clearing, hands clasped together, as if adoring the cows and heifers who were walking past him in solemn procession. When they were all inside the pen, he turned round and murmured: 'You can reassure your companion, I swear on my conscience there are no spies around this farm.'

XI

They dined in the kitchen, illuminated by a large fire. Outside all was quiet beneath a moon whose light crept over the threshold as if to lend its calm tenderness to the heated passions which reigned within.

Marianna offered bread and wine and sprinkled the salt, as on the evening of Simone's first visit. She was composed, almost stiff. Her father had offered Costantino hospitality, and it was not for her to abuse the laws of hospitality.

She was conscious of their guest's uncertainty and the ambiguous position her father found himself in, but she was waiting for the former to leave so that she could make every-thing clear. She also held her tongue because the manservant had now joined them and was looking on with a curiosity he sought to disguise. And it was he who first raised his head at the sound of horse's hooves in the distance.

'It must be Sebastiano.'

And Marianna opened her eyes wide, but quickly collected herself.

She had not seen Sebastiano for a long time. And now here he was, reappearing just when fate seemed to have settled everything. The thudding of hooves on the grass approached with the sound of the first heavy raindrops of a storm.

In a short while he was at the door; and his shadow and that of his horse obscured the threshold, blocking the gentle glow of the moon. The barking of the dogs broke the calm tranquillity of the night.

Marianna did not move. But she sat bolt upright in her chair, hostile. Her eyes, meeting Costantino's questioning glance, shone with such a steely gleam that the bandit had the impression of a glittering weapon being drawn.

Sebastiano entered and at the father's invitation took a seat at the dinner-table. He was pale, more so than usual, as if the moonlight had coloured his face.

He did not want to eat anything, but signalled the others to continue their meal; nor would he even accept any wine.

'Are you all right?' zio Berte asked.

'No, I'm not,' he answered, staring at each of those present in turn, to ensure they all understood the reason why. But only Marianna responded to his stare, fixing on him her own glittering gaze.

He nodded at her: yes. Yes, he had come to do battle. If she had changed, if she had cast off the soft vestments of a wise and gentle woman and in a seeming fit of madness had armed herself and was ready to do damage, then he too had changed, he too was armed. And his strength was doubled, like a convulsive fever, by the grievance that afflicted him. If only they had been alone! He felt capable of seizing her by the waist, bending her over his knee like a reed and snapping her in two.

The peaceful way the men were eating their dinner, talking of mundane matters, pasturage and cattle, began to exasperate him. He had not even asked who the guest was, and looked at him with indifference, mingled with a touch of scorn, as if he were the servant of some neighbouring sheep farmer. Marianna cleared the table, taking away the bread and serving dishes. Then he smacked his hand on his knee to call himself back to the purpose of his visit and shook his lowered head several times, amazed at these trivial goings-on. Then he said to the serving man: 'Go and see if my horse is eating,' and the serving man understood that he was required to leave, even though accustomed to taking part in all his master's affairs.

Marianna also made as if to go; he twisted round, stiff in his chair, frowning.

'Marianna! You stay here, because we need to speak.'

She stopped but did not sit down. Costantino, his elbow on his knee and his head propped on one hand, seemed withdrawn into himself, detached from the others like the guest whose mind is on his own affairs. Zio Berte, however, could smell the coming storm and his heart beat like a woman's. He couldn't tell whether it was for joy at the hope that his daughter's fate might be changing or from fear of the sad things which he felt, deep down, were inevitably coming.

He did not greatly trust Marianna, and still less did he trust Costantino, presently so quiet and good-natured. There he sat, as peaceful as a little old man dozing after a good meal:

touch him and he'll leap up as ferocious as a wild beast woken in its lair.

'Marianna,' he said, trying to conjure the storm away, 'what about pouring your cousin a drink?'

'He doesn't want one! So leave him be!'

'Then sit down. We'll drink, won't we, Costantino Moro? Come on, there's time enough to sleep. Pick up your cup, man, have a drink!'

Costantino sat up straight, rubbing his eyes.

'Yes, heavens, I really was dropping off... I'm tired, God help me!'

Then Sebastiano became aggressive.

'Ah, yes, you've been walking today. The go-between's job is even more exhausting than the bandit's.'

Costantino placed his horn cup on the ground. He set it, still full, on the hearthstone and the wine's surface glinted like a bloodshot eye.

'What do you mean?'

'You know exactly what I mean.'

'I don't know anything... I don't know you. Who are you?'

He had drawn himself up and seemed to have filled out, grown bigger. Inside, he felt inclined to laugh, thinking that Sebastiano was arriving on the battlefield a bit late and the combatants were already dead. But he did not hesitate for a second to defend Simone's dignity and was not going to allow either his partner or himself to be insulted.

From where she stood, Marianna looked at him warily, but also with admiration, almost encouraging him to defend himself. Her father, meanwhile, having emptied his wine in a nervous gulp, nudged her between the shoulders with the cup, but she did not take it.

So zio Berte ended up putting the horn cup on the floor as well, but to one side; then he moved Costantino's further away as if clearing the ground for a fight. His hand trembled slightly. He tried to say reprovingly: 'Sebastiano, Sebastiano!' but his voice was lost in the rising squall.

'Who am I?' Sebastiano retorted loudly, folding his arms over his chest. 'I am a man.'

And the other man guffawed.

'For heaven's sake, I can see you're a man!'

'You can cut out the sneering! It doesn't suit you, a man they say goes praying every day in churches half way up the mountains. You should listen instead. Why are you here?'

'What has my business got to do with you? And why are you here?'

'I am here because there is a woman to defend.'

'And who is abusing this woman?'

'You! You are abusing her! What were you after when you went to her house in Nuoro this morning? And what have you come here for now? Why doesn't he come himself, your partner, instead of sending you as his messenger? Ah, he's scared now, our man of honour, he's scared... the woman's not alone any more, he can't get at her so easily.'

Costantino was already on his feet, but he saw Marianna standing across from him, pale, her lips trembling uncontrollably, and he sat down again, suddenly calm, ironic.

'All right, since you're so brave, why don't you go and tell him these things to his face instead of saying them to me?'

'But aren't you his messenger? Yes, I'm saying them to

you; but be in no doubt, I will say them to him as well. I'll make sure there's an opportunity. And here's something else you can say to him: tell him to remember what he used to be, and not to believe his condition has changed. Marianna Sirca isn't for the likes of him. He is always going to be her servant. And if she has lost her sense of what's right, there are other people, by God, who haven't…'

Then Marianna doubled up and lurched forward, as if she was about to fall; her fists were knotted and her knees shaking.

'Father,' she shouted. 'Tell him to shut up, tell him to go away!'

Zio Berte waved his hands to calm everyone down.

'Come on, come on, let's stop this! These are family matters, we'll sort them out between ourselves.'

'You!' Sebastiano turned on him with contempt. 'It's not likely your daughter can rely on you to sort things out. And as for you, cousin, send me away if you like, call your serving man and set the dogs on me. But I'll defend you just the same, against yourself, because that's what we do with people who have lost their reason. And now you listen to me too. Listen, all of you! Shouting won't do any good. But I'm sending a message to Simone Sole: never to come anywhere near you again in your life, Marianna Sirca. Otherwise, by this sign of the holy cross, I'll slaughter him like a wild boar, like a fox who gets into the farmyard.'

He pulled off his cap and sketched a big sign of the cross over the fire, dividing the flames with his hand. Marianna had drawn herself up again, stiff and proud.

'And I tell you, Sebastiano Sirca, that your words are no more to me than a puff of wind.'

'Very well then! But watch out for yourself, woman. And I turn to you again, Costantino Moro, the man they say believes in God. You try to put these things right; if not, maybe you'll be answering before the Lord for what happens.'

Costantino continued to look at him with an expression of irony.

'Before the Lord I will answer for my crimes, not yours! And don't think Simone is going to be frightened of a man like you. Why do you want to be the master of everyone's destiny?'

'This is your response?'

'For now, yes. Then I'll give you my response to the words you have directed at me. At the moment we are in another person's house. So this is what we'll do: we'll go away to somewhere that is not part of Marianna Sirca's land and I'll be better able to respond to your questions.'

Marianna said: 'Nobody, either in my house or out there, has the right to discuss my business. I am the mistress, I repeat, and not even my father who is here now can command me.'

Zio Berte nodded his head, then became solemn and sad.

Sebastiano had risen to his feet, accepting Costantino's invitation. They stared at each other across the hearth like two mortal enemies, two men who had never met before and had nothing personal between them. Suddenly, however, Costantino turned his head and seemed, in the ominous silence that had developed, to be listening to the fire crackling at his feet.

'No, I have nothing more to say to you, for now. If God wills it, we shall meet again,' he said calmly.

Sebastiano did not insist. He went and fetched his horse, mounted it and came back past the kitchen; once again his shadow obscured the clear light from the moon. Then the sound of his horse's hooves echoed for a long time in the serenity of the night.

Marianna had taken her seat again. Against her will, tears of anguish and fear spilled from her eyes. Costantino poked the fire, and in leaning forward his rosary — a small red rosary that looked as if it were made of holly berries — fell from his belt and rattled on the hearthstone.

The slight noise seemed to wake everyone up. Zio Berte clasped his hands between his knees, and while Costantino picked the rosary up, murmured: 'The trouble is, we're forgetting God and forgetting that we must die. Marianna, my daughter, listen to me: I have a feeling there's death in the air and I can speak to you frankly of earthly things. Listen, Marianna, do not ruin two Christian souls. Because, you see, Simone can still save himself, and Sebastiano too, if you wish it. Instead you wish their ruin. Marianna, we all must die; life is as short as the path from this house to that tree out there, whereas eternal life is everything.'

'I can do nothing about it,' Marianna said. 'I know, agreed: life is short, yes. But that's the very reason why its little road has to be taken in one go, without turning round. For what comes after, God is the only judge.'

Then the father turned to Costantino.

'What do you say about it? You believe in God.'

'I also believe he is the only judge; it's what I too have always thought. Marianna, why don't you tell your father the truth?'

Then she stood up and said in a resolute voice: 'Father, it's all over between Simone and me.'

And she went into her bedroom, shut herself inside and stood leaning at the window. The moon was shining in a sky as pure and blue as summer dawns and every blade of grass exhaled its sweetest odour. And yet, from time to time the nightingale's call seemed like the lamentation of the earth's own heart, grieving amid all this tranquillity over a secret and incurable source of distress. And Marianna thought that she too must therefore conceal her distress in the same manner, hide it away behind the outward appearance of joy and good fortune that life had given her. She thought she should live and die like this, without lifting so much as the hem of the veil on the mysterious face of happiness.

And she felt strong, sustained from head to foot by a rigid rod of pride; but from time to time there flashed before her, with the moonbeams through the tree branches, the memory of Simone's eyes, and there came to her ears the echo of his vain promises. Then all her deepest feeling surged up inside, grief battled against pride with the force of a stormy sea crashing against a fragile paling. And her tears fell on the windowsill and from there rebounded on to the grass of the meadow, mingling with the tears of dew which the night spilled on to the bosom of the earth.

XII

Costantino followed the same route to return to their refuge as that taken by Simone a year before. Around him was the same serene moonlight, the same spring sweetness. He did not walk tall and strong, however, like his companion: he crept along slowly, head down, no taller than a small boy. There was no risk, for he still had his safe-conduct pass, but at the same time he was wary of being followed and watched. And he was burdened by the weight of Marianna's unhappiness and the humiliating word she had bidden him carry back to Simone.

He felt like a poor servant of little account, obliged by his master to take an insulting present to someone and then to bring back a still more offensive one.

But there were moments when the memory of Sebastiano's insults stung him to the quick. They brought him to a standstill, and like his companion, he felt the stirring inside him, deep inside, of a wild beast urging him to turn round, seek out Sebastiano and ram back down his throat, along with his blood, the foolish words and the vainglorious challenges.

'He dares talk to me like that? To me? Swaggering fool! You wait, you scoundrel, just you wait,' he said out loud, shaking a menacing fist at the shadows of the bushes.

Then he calmed down; he seemed to hear something like a distant whispering of prayer; and it was the very silence of the night which wrapped itself around him and carried him onward like a wave, leaving his troubles in the background. So he walked and walked, like a somnambulist, along the narrow grey paths through the silvered grasses and the shadows cast by the flowering trees and bushes. And Marianna and Simone and their passion, more filled with hate than love, seemed immensely distant, at the opposite ends of the earth; and Sebastiano's silly show of wrath too, and his own feelings of humiliation and bitterness — all of it seemed mere shadows.

But it only took the sound of a footstep far away, a pebble rattling down the hillside, a bird ruffling its feathers in its sleep, and he too started and felt ruffled all over again.

He arrived before dawn. Simone was not there. He had left the rope tied to the hook as well, and from the greasy fumes coming from the ashes of the fire and the scattered bones of what had been a meal, Costantino could tell that other companions had been there, feasting or plotting, during his absence. He sat down wearily before the embers of the fire, a surge of anger again giving way gradually to a feeling of great sadness. And he began a conversation with Marianna, as if she had followed him up here and was listening to him in the darkness of the cave.

'You see? I deceived you. And who knows whether you would have uttered that word if you had known the full truth! Who knows anything, ever? You believed Simone was leaving you out of love, out of weakness, and in fact, he's leaving you out of vanity or to prove his courage, perhaps... who knows anything, ever? Meanwhile, I didn't tell you everything, poor woman. I didn't tell you that those three men who were here a year ago came looking for Simone again, flattering him and praising him. And the youngest one, Bantine Fera, laughed, knowing Simone was in love, and he spat as a sign of contempt when he knew Simone wanted to get married in secret and hand himself over to the law. That's why Simone is leaving you, because he's ashamed of being in love. Well, I had something to say about that, a fine piece of sermonising for him: Simone, look to your conscience, Simone, don't bring misery on a woman who loves you. But it didn't do any good. While we were alone, just the two of us, he could look me in the face and laugh at me and my sermons. He is the strong one, or thinks he is, and he pays heed to no one's desires but his own. But when the other one came, Bantine Fera, who is stronger than he is, he folded. But to pretend, even if only to himself, that he's strong, he pulled out the usual excuse: he didn't know how it had happened, that he'd been bewitched, that you had bewitched him, but that now he wanted to be strong, free, full of spirit. Since Bertine Fera once abandoned a woman — who wasn't worth the nail clipping from your little toe, Marianna! — he's going to abandon you too. And he loves you, Marianna! How could anyone not love you? If the giants came down from the mountains they would kneel at your feet. But he wants to imitate Bantine Fera. And he overdoes it. His way of imitating him is to run in front of him the way a dog runs on ahead of a horse and rider!'

And Marianna was there, quiet and pale, her face buried in her hands, softly repeating her words: 'You can tell him from me that he is a coward.'

'I'll tell him all right, yes!'

He realised that the courage to speak plainly to his partner came not from his conscience but from his anger at finding he was not there, waiting for him; from knowing that he was with this other friend, a man who had become their master, the strongest of all of them. And he turned aside and curled up, surrendered to a new misery on his own account. Then sleep overtook him.

Simone was not far away. For the first time since they had met, he had not done Bantine Fera's bidding and accompanied him on his latest enterprises. Bantine Fera was the true bandit, all of a piece, brutal and without conscience. He strode unswervingly towards his objective. What he wanted, he wanted, regardless of the consequences. He had killed to avenge himself for a perceived affront; he robbed people and continued to kill not because he believed it his right but because his instinct told him to. He was the youngest of his companions and he led them, dominated them.

To avoid him, since he was waiting for Costantino's return, Simone had pretended to be ill. And he was ill, in fact: from irresolution, from love, from remorse. He had climbed up amongst the rocks above the cave and lain there, looking out for the returning Costantino. He remembered the dawn when he had returned from his visit to the Sierra, and he tried not to think about Marianna, since thinking about a woman for whom he would have to give up his own liberty was a weakness, Bantine Fera said. And rather than do that, he felt an urge to blame her, almost to hate her. It was as if she knew about some crime he had committed, and even from a distance, even though she loved him, it seemed that she dominated him and she too considered him weak and contemptible.

Then he was assailed again by thoughts of her, by desire for her.

But that only made his irritation grow. He was angry with himself. He seemed to be divided into two parts. One followed Bantine Fera in his warlike expeditions, in the quest for money and for other people's possessions, in the savage thrill of escaping ambushes. And the other part continued in its thoughts of love and grief, it crouched at Marianna's feet and wept into her lap, and in this self-humbling and this grief lay his real joy.

And the two parts of him fought each other, scorned each other, suffered, rose up and fell back defeated in the battle, tired of it all but ready to rise and fall all over again.

And so when he saw Costantino return, he did not climb down to the cave. He did not want to appear weak; he did not want to show he had been waiting. He lingered where he was for a time, his heart beating fast, hoping his partner would come looking for him. And since Costantino did not move, he began to curse him for his indifference. He decided to go down only when the dawn whitened the tops of the trees and the moon, as on that other occasion, dropped like the petals of a narcissus into the waters of the pool.

Costantino was quietly sleeping. He had his rosary twined

round his wrist and Simone took the little cross and tugged it to waken him: the limp hand lifted and seemed to wake before the rest of him.

Simone kept remembering the previous occasion, and in spite of himself, experienced a feeling of joy deep in his heart as he waited for his partner to describe Marianna's grief, and who knows, perhaps even her admiration for him. So he sat down, as befitted a strong man such as himself, with his gun at his side, his torso stiff, his hands on his knees. He resembled an idol, with his face arranged in an artificial expression of calm composure, his thick hair, crowned by the black circle of his cap, gleaming in the silvery reflections that filtered into the cave, his half-closed eyes staring down at his companion, who was gradually waking up, shivering and stretching.

A little knot of anger rose in his throat at the sight of Costantino returning so slowly and tremulously to consciousness. It seemed to Simone he was doing it on purpose, to amuse himself, but the longer it lasted, the more obstinate was his resolve to appear calm.

All at once Costantino opened his eyes wide and sat up: it was an abrupt movement, as if he meant to startle him. He tried to smile: but from Simone's serious expression he understood this was not a moment for levity. A shadow of anxiety and anger passed over his face. Simone clenched his teeth and was unable to hold himself in any more.

'What's this, did someone give you a sleeping potion? Speak, corpse.'

Costantino stared at him, as if seeing him for the first time. And indeed Simone seemed different, he seemed to have become smaller. He did not inspire fear any more, nor respect.

He was the man Marianna had exposed in a single word.

'Where were you?' he demanded, sternly.

'What business is it of yours? I'm here now. So speak. Have you seen her?'

'I have.'

'Where? In her house?'

'In her house, on the Sierra!'

'Ah, on the Sierra!' Simone said.

Shimmers of light and birdsong from outside made their fluttering way into his heart. His rigid pose dissolved a little more. He took his hands from his knees, pulled his cap further down over his brow, lowered his head.

'Why on the Sierra?' he asked quietly, as if talking to himself.

'Because she has been ill and she went to the countryside to get better.'

'Ah, she's been ill!' he said thoughtfully. But he instantly seemed to feel ashamed of his concern. 'Well!' he exclaimed, setting his hands firmly on his knees again. 'Women always have something wrong with them, or pretend they have.'

'Simone! Marianna isn't like other women, and she has no need to pretend.'

'Ah, what a fellow! It sounds as if you've fallen for her, Costantino Moro!'

'Marianna is not the woman for me.'

'As you say! Are you afraid I'll be jealous?'

'You can't be jealous, because Marianna is not the woman for you.'

Simone lowered and raised his head in a rapid gesture which was intended to convey menace, but instead conveyed surprise and offence.

'As God's my witness, you seem determined to make me angry this morning, Costantino Moro. Right, let's put an end to this because I've other more serious things on my mind. I've no time for joking. Tell me what happened.'

'There isn't much to tell you. So I went to look for her up on the Sierra. I found her, sitting quietly under the big oak in the open patch in front of the house. At first she brightened up and was full of joy to see me. Then she understood and became very quiet again… she was like a dead woman.'

'And what did she say, in the end? That's what I want to know.'

Costantino hesitated. He had a presentiment of what would happen and felt like a man standing before a pile of dry stubble with a tinder-box in his hand: it would only take a spark to set off a conflagration. And at the same time he thought it necessary to tell the truth. It was necessary and right; and often a conflagration is a good thing.

Simone, on the other hand, was growing steadily more exasperated. He sensed his companion was concealing the truth from him and wanted to assert his position as the leader.

'Well then, speak up, you wretch. I'm waiting!'

'Why this sudden urgency? You could have come down the moment you saw me come back. You were up there.'

'Yes, I was up there. Well, what does that matter? I don't have to account for my actions to you.'

'To Bantine Fera though, yes!'

'To Bantine Fera though, yes: he's a proper man, Bantine Fera, not a feeble beggar like you.'

'Well listen then. Send Bantine Fera to Marianna Sirca

and get him to bring you her reply!'

'Ah, you're making me angry. Enough!' Simone shouted, seizing a smoking log from the fire and brandishing it over him. 'If you're jealous of Bantine Fera, all right, we'll talk of that later. That's another story. Now…'

'No, it isn't another story,' Costantino said, stung into life. 'Bantine Fera and Marianna Sirca are the two arms of your cross, Simone, and they're part of the same story. He's the one who's playing the devil to get you away from her…'

'But weren't you the first one to advise me not to go with her, not to ruin myself for her?'

'And why didn't you take any notice then? No, damn it, you laughed at me, when I only had good intentions. And you went back to her, and you promised to do what she wanted, and to marry her, and you caused her to reveal her secret to everyone, and you exposed her to persecution, to ridicule, to abuse from all sides. You made her break every connection around her to be just with you, and when she only had you, you abandoned her, without a word, for the sole reason that a more powerful criminal has told you that it's shameful to love a woman and stand by her. Yes, yes, you abandoned her without a word, because you abandoned her long ago, in your mind, and she believed she was still with you and instead she was alone and you were running about doing bad things with your companion… and you didn't even have the courage to go and tell her the truth. Yes, and you sent me, the way you send a servant, the way you send a messenger boy who won't have to take the punishment. And now I'll tell you…'

He passed on word for word Sebastiano's message, but he hesitated to repeat Marianna's.

Simone, holding the smoking piece of wood in his hand, listened dumbfounded. His eyes shone with hatred: hatred for everyone; for Sebastiano, whom he had always dismissed as a person of no consequence; for Marianna, who had made him love her; for Bantine Fera, who had turned him away from her; for Costantino, who was telling him the truth. A dull rage began to make him breathe heavily: the ferocious animal inside him was stirring.

'Be quiet! You call yourself a man? You're as much use as a dead hare! Aren't you ashamed you didn't wash your snout in the fellow's blood? I don't want to hear any more. You don't know what you are!'

'It's you who don't know what you're doing and what you are,' Costantino insisted, determined, unmoving, as if resigned to the expected assault. 'You're a miserable wretch! I pity you.'

Simone started forward, waving the brand like a burning club.

'Either you hold your tongue or I'll stop your mouth with this.'

'Hit me! Go on, hit me, and then I'll give you Marianna's message, the word she sent you in reply.'

Simone lunged at him and struck him on the back of the head with the smoking brand. The sparks from the impact seemed to fly from Costantino's hair. Yet all he did was make the barest movement, tilting his head back in his habitual gesture, and instinctively putting his hand to his cap, which smelled of scorched material. And he said, without raising his voice, without getting up, without even raising his eyes, now filling with tears: 'Coward!'

Simone gave a yell and hurled himself from the cave, still

clutching the brand as if he was going to set fire to the whole world.

XIII

Towards midday the weather had turned grey, almost cold.

Marianna was sitting by the fire, as she had sat in her Nuoro house throughout the long days of winter and waiting, and once again it seemed that everything, Costantino's visit, Simone's message, Sebastiano's grotesque threats, had all been a dream.

Except that, when she stirred, raised her eyes to look through the window and saw the tree tops buffeted by the wind, it seemed now to have been Costantino's visit that had broken the peacefulness of springtime and left festering throughout the farmstead and its wider spaces all this turbulence and anguish.

Better like this, however, better to live in settled misery than in the humiliation of uncertainty and vain waiting.

She had decided to return that same day to Nuoro. But

shortly after midday, as the horse, already saddled, waited patiently beneath the oak in the clearing, the weather became even more menacing. It began to rain. The wind drove against the trees with a continuous rushing sound.

After putting the horse in the shelter, the father re-entered the house and glanced at her furtively. She was very quiet, his brave Marianna, and he understood that the drama was now over, the danger averted. And yet, he didn't know why, he was not happy. He admired her more than ever, his silent daughter, but he was not happy. He would have liked to see her cry. He stood at the window, and for a while studied the bad weather outside, his hands clasped, sad that he could do nothing against the storm. Then he set about re-boiling a piece of leather for a tobacco pouch, and after that he scraped out the hoof of a young veal calf he intended to use as a scoop for milk curds. Every now and then he looked up to gaze outside; the whole horizon now formed a single rolling cloud; the wind flattened the wet grass in the meadow, and when it sprang up again, flattened it again: it looked as if even the earth was seized by the same undulating motion.

Marianna finally stirred: she thought she had heard, through the noises of the storm, a sound of steps which her heart insisted on matching to its own increased beat. She had flushed, at first from this new turbulence, then from shame at being vulnerable to such turbulence. She would have liked to take her heart in her fist and squeeze it and wring the blood out of it like the blood-red juice of a bunch of grapes. But she still heard footsteps, and she stood on tip-toe to see better outside.

Her father suddenly noticed her restlessness.

'Don't worry about this weather,' he said timidly. 'It

won't last. And don't think of going while it's like this. Take the advice of the people who love you.'

Marianna was not even listening: she could still hear footsteps, and it felt as if someone was walking just above her head, beating down on it with insistent heels. In the end her father ceded to her his place at the window. The tall manservant came back inside as well, after putting the cattle under shelter, and he too sat down beside the fire. Rainwater dribbled from his fingers and in a short time there was a ring of dampness all round him and he was surrounded by a mist of steam from his drying clothes. For a while there was nothing to hear but the rushing of the wind and rain. No one was speaking, but from time to time, as if aware of a sense of waiting, the two men glanced at each other and then at Marianna.

Marianna remained motionless by the window. The little farm kitten had jumped on to the sill, fixing its large green eyes anxiously on the world outside. It seemed to have spotted something beyond the meadow, beyond the wood. It occasionally turned its head and stared at Marianna. Then it settled again to wait, like her. All at once it jumped down and disappeared. The dogs were barking: the rain stopped, the clouds parted; and in the greenish spaces of the sky above the wood the moon appeared.

Then Marianna saw Simone emerge from the wood and advance rapidly over the clearing as if swimming through the wet grasses still tossing in the wind. His eyes were shining in his pale face, and the muzzle of his gun glinted of its own accord, like an eye keeping watch over its master, looking out for enemies that might be following him.

Marianna retreated to the fireplace and said to the two

men: 'Don't move!' Then she went outside, closing and locking the door on them.

She also closed and locked from the outside the door to her little bedroom and stood in front of it as if to prevent Simone from entering the house. No, he must never enter it again. And the house seemed to weep tears on her, with the drops of rain still running off the roof. And everything around her still seemed to be weeping, even though the storm's fury had abated and the sky was opening like a great tear-stained eye.

Simone made straight towards her. He was streaming with water, his face distorted with tiredness and breathlessness from his long and hasty journey. But his eyes shone with an almost ferocious gleam. Marianna felt both pity and fear at the sight.

They stared at one another, as they had on that earlier occasion, looking into each other's souls. And they seemed to be equals, as they had then, equals in pride and in suffering, as they had been before, in both servitude and in love.

'Marianna,' he said, coming to a halt in front of her, so close that his wet clothes dripped their wetness on to her own. 'You said a word meant for me, a word you have to take back.'

Marianna looked at him without replying, pressing herself against the door, determined not to open it even if the man tried to harm her.

'Answer me, Marianna. Why don't you answer? You can see that I am here and that I am not a coward.'

A faint smile passed over her lips, a touch of mockery, and she looked into the distance and all around as though to see what perils he had passed through. Then he took hold of her wrists, pinning her to the door, and brought his face up to hers.

'Answer! Why did you say I was a coward? Have I done you any harm? Have I? I could have, that evening here, and then at your house, and then at anytime, anywhere, and I still could but I don't, you can see I don't. Can you see that? Answer me.'

She looked at him again, through half-closed eyes, her mouth tight, her face pale but firm.

'You don't want to respond to me! There have been other times when you've responded though. Coward, me? Coward, me? What have I asked of you that makes me a coward? Have I asked you for your money maybe? Your possessions, have I asked for those? Or have I asked you for your body? I have only asked you for love, and love you have given me. But I have given you love too. We are equal; we have exchanged our hearts. But you wanted more from me: you wanted my freedom, and that I'm not giving you, no, for heaven's sake, because I owe it to others ahead of you, I owe it to my mother, my father, my sisters... coward, me?' he went on hoarsely, driven wild with rage by her silence. 'It was you who wanted me to be a coward. You, who wanted to make me turn myself in, you who wanted to tie me to you like a dog on a leash... you...'

Suddenly he fell silent and dropped her wrists, pale, cold with dread. Marianna had closed her eyes in order not to see him, and little by little she let her back slide down the door until she let herself go altogether and dropped to a sitting position on the step; and he thought he had killed her. He crouched at her feet, as he had done before, he sat on the wet grass, took her hands again, looked pleadingly up at her.

'Marianna? Marianna? Answer me, Marianna!'

It was another man's voice, the voice of the good Simone of that other evening. But she remained silent, eyes cast down, uncertain, as shut off from his pain as she had been from his anger.

'Marianna, answer me. It's me, it's your Simone; look, I've come; I'm here; take me back; do what you want with me, Marianna, forgive me. At least tell me you forgive me.'

She did not answer. She was dead, for him. And he sensed it clearly enough, that she was dead for him, and he tugged off his cap and threw it away, pulled the gun from his shoulder and threw it down, wrung his hands in despair. He stammered meaningless words, absurd threats, curses against himself and against everyone. She remained inert, blind and dumb, dead to everything.

'After all, what have I done?' he said, gathering his wits again. He reached for his cap and pressed it down firmly over his forehead. 'It was true your house was surrounded by spies. Maybe it was my fault, yes, because as a strong man I should have kept our secret quiet, and I should have been the one to go looking for the priest, I should have, if I'd been a man of sufficient courage. Instead I sent my mother, yes, and the secret was passed on to my sisters as well, and even to the neighbours… yes, I behaved like a weak and silly woman. But even if that was my fault, your house *was* surrounded by spies, and it was my duty not to let myself get arrested in your house, not to give you that grief and that shame. You understand me, Marianna; at least say you understand me! You can see I'm speaking as if I were your own conscience! But no; you keep silent, you don't answer.'

She reopened her eyes and looked at him; and they were

calm, those eyes, as formerly, but too calm, just as if they were watching from some far off place of safety, where dispassionate judgements are made; watching from beyond.

Simone picked up his gun and laid it across his knees; then he took one of her hands again, which she let him have, cold and limp.

'You understand reason, Marianna. My poor Marianna! You see, you understand reason. And even here, on your farm, there's someone lying in wait for me, someone who means harm. At least, that's what I've been told. And that's why I didn't come. Imagine getting myself arrested, even getting myself killed, in front of you! How terrible that would be for you! Do you understand? Speak, give me just a single word. And then, you see,' he added, but bowing his head as if ashamed of his words, 'when you think about us in reality, it was a mad thing we were doing… Marianna… the sort of thing children might do… and we're not children any more… and then, there's this… the fact that you're rich and I'm poor…'

Then the life seemed to flow back into her: she reddened, and did not withdraw the hand he was gripping tightly but said quietly, in her calm voice: 'But you knew that all along. And if I was the rich person compared with you the poor person, you were the poor one compared with me the rich one…'

He reddened as well. He swallowed his saliva, disgusted, as if swallowing a bitter pill, and shook his head. He no longer understood anything, or felt he didn't: he was wearied by all the things he had said, as he was wearied by the long journey he had made; and his weariness was entirely futile; and he would have liked to rest his head in Marianna's lap once more and go to sleep.

Suddenly, though, his indignation returned. In the end, she had not withdrawn the insulting word; and she was not withdrawing it even now, seeing him at her feet, so tired and so reduced. On the contrary she was adding insult to insult. But if she no longer wished to reopen her door to him, neither did he intend to slink off like a beggar who has been refused alms. He imagined the mockery of Bantine Fera, if he had known. And the ferocious animal in him began to stir. He began to breathe heavily; he shouldered his gun again and remembered he had left the cave still holding the glowing brand with the intention of setting fire to Marianna's farm and her house and of slaughtering the cattle and killing the servants, her family and relatives, and even her, if she did not take back that word. He saw everything through a veil of red. The water that drenched his body mingled with his sweat and became warm; and he seemed to be soaked in blood, in the blood welling from the terrible wound which, with that single word, Marianna had gouged in his heart.

But the look on her face held him in check. She continued to stare at him, not speaking, her head tilted a little to the side, to the right. It was an attitude that reminded him of Costantino and it seemed to him that Marianna too knew everything, that she had followed his every step in those months of error and servitude, a thousand times worse than the servitude of old, and that she was staring at him from the depths of her knowledge. He bowed his head, and in the buzzing that filled his ears he seemed to hear a voice, which was her voice, or the voice of Costantino, or of Bantine Fera, or perhaps it was his own voice, repeating Marianna's word.

Then he leapt to his feet again, furious with himself, and

fled, running across the meadow.

And only then did Marianna begin to tremble. She believed he was running away to do himself harm and her first instinct was to follow him or shout for him to stop; but pride kept her motionless, mute, her back against the door. Suddenly, though, an inner voice began to cry out in her too, saying she had been unjust, that she had said a harsh and false thing in throwing back in Simone's face his poverty compared to her wealth. She too had been cowardly, responding to his protestations and his excuses with nothing better than an insult. So here they were, equals again. They could run as far as they liked: they were bound always to follow the same path and to find themselves side by side whenever they paused.

Meanwhile he had disappeared into the wood. The shadows of dusk seemed to close in behind him.

Marianna looked up. She saw the sky had completely cleared and was now a greenish blue, with a large, pink-tinged moon rising above trees still heavy with water. She saw the meadow before her reflecting the moonlight like the surface of a pond. In the abrupt silence she could still hear quite clearly Simone's crashing footsteps. And she followed him with anguish, convinced in her heart that he was running out of her life for ever. But all the same, in a part of her heart that was deeper still, she sensed once more that the fear he was leaving her for ever was a deception. Yes, he was running, he was fleeing; but she too was running and fleeing; their road was the same road and they must always find each other again at every stop.

She sighed deeply and went to open the kitchen door. The manservant had obeyed, and had not moved. Her father, on the other hand, had run to the window the moment she left the house, had seen Simone arrive and then go away, and now he was waiting anxiously for her to come back inside.

Seeing her pale and troubled, her eyes gleaming with tears which refused to fall, he went towards her, but did not have the courage to ask her what was happening. He merely looked at her, and felt that something terrible had already happened, worse than if Simone had attacked her, worse than if he had killed her.

Without speaking she took up her place at the window again and everything was once more silent in the dark kitchen. Her head formed a black silhouette against the green and gold of the background, with the moon to one side. The two men turned to exchange glances from time to time, with a painful sense of anticipation. Suddenly the dogs began to bark again, with loud, mournful howls, and Marianna went to the door, then returned to the window. She seemed to know what was happening outside, in the mystery of the wood, and made a sign with her hand in the direction of the dogs, as if to command them to silence so that she could hear better.

A gunshot rang out, clear, close. The echo repeated it, then a more distant second echo repeated it again.

She answered with a cry, as if to a summons.

And she ran outside again, this time followed by the men.

They found Simone beside the spring, under the over-hanging rocks, in the very place the manservant had seen him one morning the previous June, after his first visit to the farmhouse.

Leaving the house moments before her father and the servant and running ahead of them into the wood like a wounded deer in her breathless search, it was Marianna who saw him first. He was on his knees at the spring, his hands pressed against the stone at its side; he seemed to be trying to lever himself to his feet. The muzzle of his gun, still standing upright over his shoulder, glistened in the moonlight, keeping watch, uselessly now, over its wounded master.

Marianna did not cry out. She took him by the shoulders to help him stand; he let himself go, sinking back into her arms and she cradled him, falling back under his weight to sit on the stone.

They were together once more: his blood trickled over her apron; and searching for the wound with her hand, she felt blood run warm between her fingers, and had the impression Simone was leaking it from everywhere.

'Simone, Simone!'

He seemed to have let himself fall back against her on purpose and was making an offering of his blood as he had promised on that evening.

Then she started to call out in terror.

The men came running up at once: they lifted Simone and carried him back to the house. Blood dripped all over the grass. Marianna, following closely in their steps, her hands clasped to her forehead, felt entirely covered in blood, from the soles of her feet to the roots of her hair.

And her door was opened once more to Simone.

The men laid him on her little bed and began to undress him. He appeared to be sleeping, his hair still wet with rain, in exhausted abandon on the pillow. And he let them do as they pleased. He allowed his gun, which never left his side, to be taken away, the bandolier of cartridges, his belt, his cap and his outer coat. As the men handed her each object and item of clothing, Marianna laid them on the bench. And involuntarily, despite the terror of the moment, it came into her head that one day he would have had to strip himself like this in order to belong to her. This was it then, their nuptials finally come to pass: nuptials of death. And yet deep down, somewhere below the depths of her heart, in another realm of profundity, she sensed that their true union was this: they belonged to each other in death, in eternity.

His chest was revealed, as white as a woman's, his finely muscled side spotted with little brown moles. The wound was there, between two ribs; a small red hole. Blood continued to flow from it, as calmly and steadily as the water from the spring.

The servant bent down to look, with the expert eye of a doctor; he took the lips of the wound between two fingers, pinching them hard, while with his free hand he helped the master to turn Simone's body to lie straight on its other side.

'The wound won't be fatal if the bullet hasn't lodged inside. Give me some vinegar, Marianna.'

Marianna poured vinegar into a jar; and her tears mingled with it; she passed it over with one hand while holding the light up with the other and murmured falteringly as she looked at Simone's face: 'We have killed him, and we're pouring vinegar into his wound just as they did to Christ...'

Only then did zio Berte, who up to that moment had seemed a different man, firm and resolute, give a great sigh and clasp his hands together.

'Ah, Sebastiano, what have you done!'

Afterwards, no one spoke any more. In the silence, all

that could be heard was the rasp of linen as Marianna tore up a sheet to make bandages and — from outside — the song of a nightingale.

While the two men came and went, saying nothing, trying to obliterate the traces of blood, Marianna sat by the little bed. Simone appeared still to be sleeping. She talked to him softly, touching his inert hand. With her eyes half-blinded from weeping, she could see nothing of what was happening around her. But inside she could see with utmost clarity into every corner, to those realms of profundity beneath the depths of the heart, into that hidden place where knowledge of the truth radiates light like a treasure in an underground vault.

'I have killed you,' she said to Simone, touching his fingers one by one, and the hollow of his palm, still slightly warm. 'My pride has killed you. Forgive me. Don't go away like this; don't do as I did, go silent, say only cruel words. Forgive me: and don't speak, no, if you don't want to. I know all the same, Simone, my sweetheart. You gave me so much; you gave me love; not your love for me, no, I don't mean that, but my love for you, my love. It was a great treasure, and I didn't know how to care for it. Because someone who has always been poor, like me, doesn't know the value of things: and so I squandered it, the treasure you had given me. I let it all go, I threw it from the windows of my house! It is only justice, now, that you should go away. Because you have nothing left; we have nothing left, Simone, my sweetheart. And I wanted still more, from you. You were right when you told me so. I wanted your freedom as well, and I wanted to be married, wretch that I was, I wanted the ring on my finger, from you, the ring that doesn't exist except at the end of the rainbow. Mercy on me, I wanted your blood, your life: and now you have given them to me, as you had promised, your blood and your life, Simone, my sweetheart. They were right, your sisters, to be wary of me.'

At the memory of his sisters, their strength of character, she could no longer restrain herself and began to cry again. But in that very anguish she found a sense of relief, and it seemed to her that her tears, falling on the face and hands of Simone, might succeed in bringing him back to life. And indeed, he faintly moved the tips of his fingers.

She sat up straight, looked afresh at everything around her, the small and lonely room lit by the little lamp, his clothes on the bench, the gun in the corner, his face, pale, lying on the pillow, its eyes open, astonished. It seemed he was waking from a deep dream and struggling to remember.

'Marianna?' he called softly.

XIV

Meanwhile Sebastiano was pacing through the wood, on the way back to his own sheepfolds. He was panting, and his heart was still beating fast, but he convinced himself he was well satisfied; in any event, he had been alert and prompt to act. He had kept his promise: after sending Simone a message not to come anywhere near Marianna again unless he was prepared to pay for his temerity with his blood, he had not gone far from the farmstead. He waited; he already knew what was bound to happen. And here he was, Simone, arriving at a run, and after some talk with Marianna, departing at a run, like a man who hasn't enough time to do all the things destiny has in store for him. A shot, and there he was, halted in his tracks, for ever.

Sebastiano was not certain he had killed him. That, though, was not of prime importance to him: the essential thing was that he had kept his promise. And while he walked, the silence of the wood barely broken by the murmur of a distant mountain torrent, he too talked to his victim.

'You see, young man? You believed you could charge ahead, chest puffed out, and sweep all before you, and instead you've been knocked flat and deflated. That'll teach you. You're young and you'll learn. Didn't my message warn you that Marianna has other relatives, even if her father's a simpleton? Now you've seen. God's my witness, now you've seen.'

As he walked on, his sense of anxiety diminished.

'Why am I making off like this?' he asked himself. 'I don't want to hide, I want to pay; I want to pay my dues. No, I've no desire to hide, I'm not a coward, not me!'

He stopped abruptly, as if the victim, lying prone at his feet, were blocking his way.

He pulled his gun from his shoulder, looked long and hard at the ground before him. The moon was crossing the lonely sky and sending its mournful light through the forest trees. The murmur of the swollen torrent receded, and from the grey holm oaks, seemingly made of stone, not of wood, drops of water fell and ran lightly over his face and hands.

He began to walk again, but no longer with the same feeling of satisfaction. He was thinking of Marianna, of her fright and pain on finding Simone dead or wounded. And he imagined he could hear the shout, a shout that dealt him a blow between the shoulders and drove him onward in his flight. But at the same time it had the effect of a noose thrown from a long distance, tightening round his neck, tugging him backwards.

She was shouting after him: 'Coward, coward!'

He stopped again.

'Me, a coward? Me, risking my life and liberty to defend you?'

He walked on; but indignation made him bend at the knees and stumble. He raised his head, craning his neck back as if that noose really was tugging at him, suffocating him. He struggled on in this fashion for some distance, and the further he went, the more ashamed he felt to have fled the scene. He turned back a few steps; stopped again; no longer knew whether he should press on or go back; felt the shame involved in doing either. In the end he slumped to the ground, sitting with his back to a tree trunk, and sighed heavily. He was the defeated one, the wounded one, he felt it clearly; yet he also felt a sense of relief at letting go like this.

The clot of bile that had built up in his heart during all this period of hatred was dissolving, seeping away through the wound. He couldn't tell why, but he no longer hated. Marianna's grief and Simone's blood repaid his own long grief, his humiliation. He was calm now, like a satisfied creditor.

Yet after a moment's respite, all his emotion came flooding back. Deep down, he had not abandoned his feelings for Marianna. He believed he had been sincere in thinking he must defend her against herself; and now he could see her crouched over Simone, earnestly trying to raise him up, to call him back to life. He jumped to his feet and returned the way he had come.

All was quiet under the light of the moon. The sound of the torrent came only feebly, as if the water had gone to sleep and was murmuring in its dreams; and on Marianna's farmstead the nightingale never ceased its singing.

He circled the pool, imagining he might find Simone still

lying at the spot where he had fallen. And he was amazed at the silence that had gathered round it. The ground seemed to have swallowed up the victim, concealing him so as not to disturb the peace of the night.

Further on, however, as he emerged from the wood, he saw lights in the windows of the farmhouse and dark figures moving about.

'He's there, alive, he's more alive than ever!'

And he felt that his hatred and his vendetta had been no more than a vain struggle against the will of destiny.

He went rapidly up to the house. The men were in the kitchen waiting for Marianna's orders. Outside, the horse was saddled and ready to leave and the servant had spurs on his boots, while zio Berte was vaguely wringing his hands, uncertain whether he should be the one to go to find Simone's parents or whether he should remain with his daughter.

When he saw Sebastiano walk in, an initial spurt of anger led him to approach and seize him by the folds of his cloak. But that face, pale and waxen, the eyes grave and despairing, forced him to check his words.

'Is he through there?' Sebastiano asked. 'Is he very bad?'

He looked penitent, his arms hanging at his sides, his head bowed.

'The wound may not be very serious. But the bullet is still inside, deep inside… Sebastiano, why did you do this?'

'Because I had to do it!'

'Listen to me, then: you have done something senseless. Everything was over between Marianna and Simone.'

Sebastiano stared, then closed his eyes. Then he tried to justify himself by denial.

'It isn't true! Why do you say that?'

'I say it because it's the truth. Marianna and Simone had separated.'

Sebastiano went to sit by the hearth, his gun still slung over his shoulder. He put his elbows on his knees and his face between his fists as if trying to crush his jawbones; and both fists and jaws were shaking with rage.

'It isn't true, it isn't true…' he said at intervals.

The servant, perfectly calm, said to his master: 'Since Sebastiano's here, one of us can go.'

So zio Berte went through to his daughter. Simone had only just regained consciousness and was looking round, trying to raise his head. Marianna had taken his hand and was squeezing it, anxiously waiting for him to speak again. But his eyes clouded over, his head fell back heavily on the pillow, and the sleep of death which he had barely shaken off overwhelmed him once more.

'Marianna,' her father said, touching a finger to her shoulder, 'we need to decide what to do.'

She started.

'You do whatever is necessary.'

And zio Berte turned away.

'He's come round but he's delirious. He's burning with fever. We need to let his people know.'

'What did the mistress say?' the servant asked, bending down to fasten a spur.

'She didn't say anything. But we've no need for orders in this situation. Go straight to Simone's house and tell them how things stand. Away!'

'I'd prefer it if… the mistress decided.'

222

But for the first time since he had been in service there, he saw zio Berte lose his temper.

'I am the master here! Be on your way, and stop playing the idiot. Go!'

So he obeyed, and in a short time the rapid drumming of horse's hooves could be heard disappearing into the distance. Only then did Sebastiano raise his head and sit up straight; and it seemed he wanted to ask something; then he huddled into himself again and spoke no more.

At dawn, Simone's mother arrived, riding behind the servant on his horse. Her body was stooped, her head covered by a black scarf, her face already pale from its long imprisonment in grief. She slid down from the horse even before the man had dismounted and made her way directly to the room where her son lay. Marianna stood up to surrender her place. They said no word to each other; but from that moment the mother never left Simone's side; she held his hand between hers, bending over him as Marianna had done to speak to him quietly, saying to him all the things which for a long time had not been said, while Marianna came and went, moving about the little room on tip-toe and every now and then halting at the foot of the bed as if awaiting some order.

And in fact the mother, realising that the fever was rising and the wounded man was losing the strength to speak even incoherently, looked up and said: 'I want a priest here, to administer the Sacraments.'

A priest! Marianna went to give the orders: only then did she see Sebastiano. Her eyes widened, and finding herself unable to speak, she gestured with her hand for him to leave. He was not looking at her though, sitting motionless and waxen-featured, his eyes fixed on some indeterminate point, and she dropped her head and two large tears ran down her cheeks and fell to the floor.

Then abruptly she shook herself. She seemed to be confronted by a mountain whose sides were marble-smooth, impossible to scale. It was useless to weep, useless to cry out, useless to seek revenge: everything was useless.

There was Sebastiano before her, more wounded, closer to death than Simone. With her feeble hands she could bind him and turn him over to the justice of man, she could even kill him, there at her feet, like a rabid dog; the weight of her grief would not be diminished by a single gram.

So she walked over to him and touched his shoulder, as her father had touched hers. He turned his eyes and looked at her, without speaking. His pupils dilated as he stared into her own. It seemed as though he had suddenly understood the full gravity of his evil action and was overwhelmed by the horror of it.

'Sebastiano,' she said, crying again, 'this is the second time I have asked you to go away. Go: do you understand? And never set foot in my house again...'

He stood up, adjusted the gun on his shoulder, and went out. But when he came to the pool and the spot where Simone had fallen, he could not go on. He sat down, and set himself to wait again.

From there, he saw zio Berte mount the horse and ride off towards Nuoro. Everything around the farm was quiet and still. The herd was grazing, the grey cows amid the long grass looking like rocks against the blue backdrop that showed between one cork oak and the next. The sharp calls of the magpies, imitating the alarm calls of the blackbirds, cut like silver threads through the silence of the wood, and the smoke rose vertically from the farmhouse, spilling out high above like the head of a vast oat stalk.

Everything seemed a dream. Only the dogs became excited, rearing on their hind legs and pulling at the rope that tied them to the tree, barking at length at the kitten which had silently come to dip its nose in the water bowl.

And the shadows gradually lengthened over the land again. The mother was still at the bedside and had already told Simone everything there was to say. She had told him how the news of the disaster had come as a surprise neither to her, nor the father, nor the sisters.

For a long time they had all felt, like an unacknowledged illness at the bottom of their hearts, that they were waiting for a piece of news like this. And now, with the arrival of Marianna's servant, they had looked into each other's faces, as if to say with their eyes: 'It has happened.'

'We looked at each other, Simone, and immediately I bound a scarf round my head to come to you. Your sisters and your father are constantly being watched. And all the people to do with the law know them: if one of them came they would have been followed and would have discovered where you were hiding. Everyone has forgotten my face, since I haven't left the house for years now, you know that… for many years… since you went away… and so I have come, since it was up to me to see you. And here you are… bleeding and out of your senses and making the same little cries and moans as the day you were born.'

Marianna came and went in silence, without hope; except

that she was jealous of the mother who had come and separated them one more time; and she watched for the moment when she could repossess her place at his side.

Towards evening, seeing no sign of her father returning from his journey to Nuoro in search of the priest, she gazed out from the doorway, then stepped out and made her way towards the wood, down along the clear little path through the already darkening grasses.

There was no one to be seen. It was a soft, luminous evening; the whole farm, washed and refreshed by the storm of the previous day, smelt like a bunch of lavender. And the stars were appearing, one after the other, each larger and brighter than the one before as if they were vying in beauty.

She walked on, pale once again, slightly stooping, looking slightly older, as she had on that first occasion when she had come up to the farm to restore herself after her uncle's death. She walked a good distance, as far as a piece of high ground from where the main road was visible.

The woods behind her looked like the sea, with their great green swaying tops; at her feet stretched the lowland table, still green and blue in the falling dusk, with low walls, rocks, bushes of scrub in flower. The mountains seemed to evaporate on the horizon, still red from the setting sun, but covered in an ashy veil. The moon rose white over Orthobene, and across this immensity, all was peace.

Marianna remained on this high ground as an hour passed, leaning against a stone. She felt suddenly calm, detached from the things that had brought her so much suffering. There were moments when even the knowledge that Simone and his mother were in her house, temporary masters of it all, faded into oblivion. She was far away; she had left everything behind, she was naked, suspended in space like the moon.

But the sound of horses' hooves on the path recalled her to reality. She made her way down, stumbling between the stones, and arrived in the clearing at the same moment as her father and the priest.

XV

The priest was a sturdy young man, dark-complexioned, whose white teeth gleamed between prominent lips. He was well wrapped up in a bright cloak and wearing a little skull-cap instead of the tricorn hat, which made him look like a priest from Abyssinia.

He also had two brothers who were themselves absconders from justice, and could not deny his help to a dying man.

Marianna nodded to him in greeting and led him into the little bedroom. The mother had lit the brass lamp hanging from a hook in the wall above the bed. A round shadow, slowly oscillating, covered the wounded man's face like a shroud, and the ring of light, dimmed by the last glow of dusk, rose to play against the reed-covered ceiling.

Simone was dozing and appeared, beneath that shadowy veil, already to have surrendered to the calm slumber that precedes death.

The priest advanced cautiously to stand beside the mother, looking down on him in silence. The mother had risen and she too looked down at him with infinite pity, fearful that Simone might wake from his brief moment of calm, fearful that he might not wake again.

Then she moved aside and the priest sat by the bed, praying.

The women withdrew and went outside to wait. And Marianna, more tired than ever, ready to sleep, thought of Jesus in the Garden of Olives, and was afraid to let sleep overcome her. She felt as if a shadowy veil had fallen across her face as well, yet she could see a light in the distance.

'What shall I do, now?' she thought.

She would not love again, she would not wait again. But her feeling was not one of despair; rather it was a feeling of hope and rest: henceforth Simone could run into no further dangers.

She would no longer hear his footstep on the earth; but it was he, now, who must hear her footstep on the earth, and wait for her on that margin where true freedom begins.

In the kitchen, meanwhile, the servant and the master were preparing a supper. Even in houses that death has come to visit, the living must feed themselves; and then the priest was young, he had made a difficult journey, and it was right to honour him as the extraordinary guest he was. So zio Berte was crouching over the fire, blowing it into life, every now and then lifting his cap from his thin hair, and the servant, as on the first evening when Simone had come to the farmhouse, was preparing the meat for roasting, his hands red with blood.

His face remained closed, impassive. And even the master's gradually began to clear: after all God knows what he is about, and his ways are inscrutable to men. And the person who coined the proverb "every cloud has a silver lining" was certainly someone who, like all coiners of proverbs, had a long experience of life.

He beckoned the servant closer, and nodding towards the window, in the direction of the wood, he said in an undertone: 'That idiot is still there, by the spring. We should at least take him something to drink.'

'Better to think of the women' the servant muttered. 'They've been fasting all day, as if it was Good Friday.'

'We'll think of them all. Have a little patience, man!'

He straightened up, leaning his hands on his knees, breathing heavily. Since the priest had entered the house he had been experiencing a sense of relief. It seemed to him that all these things were turning out for the best and little by little returning to normal, the way they once used to be.

So he sent the servant out to look for Sebastiano, then prepared the table. Here was the jug of curds, here was the honeycomb on a cork-wood tray. Riding past his daughter's house he had been mindful to call in and get Fidela to give him some of the white bread; and here was the new cheese, pale and damp as beeswax, and here was the wine too. Everything was here: it might have been a wedding banquet. The kitten followed at his heels, rubbing itself against the coarse fabric of his gaiters, whose slightly abrasive surface brought a voluptuous glow to the kitten's large green eyes. Suddenly, though, it squealed and leapt away. The master had trodden on its little paw. Hearing the squeal, Marianna, outside, started and woke up again. The moon was rising over the wood, the whole sky was as blue as day, and everything stood out brightly in the clearing. A man was striding towards the house, straight through the grasses of the meadow; and she recognised him immediately.

'It's Costantino, his partner,' she said quietly to Simone's mother. 'He clearly knew he was coming here, and when he didn't return, he must have set out to look for him.'

Costantino came to a halt in front of them and Marianna stood up to receive him. They looked at one another, as they had the first time, in the bright moonlight, and they understood each other.

'He's inside,' she said, turning her pale face towards the bedroom. 'He's mortally wounded and he's lost consciousness. The priest's here.'

Costantino, as well, seemed relieved to know the priest was with him. He laid a gentle hand on the head of Simone's mother and felt it hot beneath his fingertips. And at this contact the woman's grief seemed finally to be released: she took Costantino's hand, sobbing, and bathed it with her tears.

Then they were all reunited in the kitchen.

Zio Berte and the servant had helped Simone's mother in, almost carrying her; and Marianna, summoning her own remaining strength, served her with the food.

The priest sat down amongst them. He was the only one who occasionally allowed himself to say a few words, but soon his voice was lost into the silence of the others. Besides, there was something religious about that supper, in that circle of people, each bowed under their own particular burden of distress, but united in a common thought that silence was the better part. And they were silent, and it seemed that they were taking communion before preparing themselves to witness the mystery of a human death.

Almost all of them, in addition, had an unspoken fear that some officer of the law might arrive from Nuoro and disturb the mystery: at every unexpected noise they raised their heads and listened.

Every now and then Marianna rose from the table to go and look at Simone, still in a semi-conscious doze. Finally she saw his eyes open again and look at her with a gleam of light that soon faded.

'Simone? Simone?'

He made an effort to sit up; he fell back, his face expressing frustration and disgust. He had the impression of being pinned to the bed by a spear that had been driven through his side. And it seemed that his body was spinning round and round with the spear as its axis. He clutched at Marianna's hand to steady himself, but she began to spin round with him.

'Simone? Simone? The priest is here. Do you want him?'

He focussed his eyes on her again, the pupils dilated, transfixed with terror. A priest? He did not understand.

'Do you want him? It's Father Fenu, he's the brother of Giacomo and Giovanni Fenu.'

He nodded yes, but turned his head a little tiredly on the pillow and she saw something like a rose appear on the material under the corner of his mouth; it was blood. She stood up in fright. But he would not let go of her hand; he seemed to want to take her with him, on the journey he was making. He began to mumble incoherently again.

'The priest... the ring... the rainbow. Mother, give me

my knapsack…'

Marianna turned her head away to the wall and felt her insides quake, but it seemed as if Simone was squeezing her hand to remind her of her promise.

'A woman who loves a man like me must not weep.'

The priest resumed his place at the bedside and found himself superimposing on the bandit's face the face of a barbarian Christ. He thought of his brothers, Giacomo and Giovanni, lost among the woods and stony places, hunters and prey at the same time. And from the depths of his heart he absolved Simone as he might absolve a little boy at his first confession.

And Simone, amid his fevered dreams, forced himself to recall, to summon together all his sins. But they escaped him, whirling round as if already detached from him, passing and repassing before him, mocking him. He murmured fractured words. Then he fell silent and seemed to be going to sleep. But hearing the priest utter the words for the absolution, he made a great effort to rouse himself, grabbed at the sheets, seemed to be trying to push against the bed and half-raised himself, with his mouth again filled with blood and frustrated disgust.

The priest laid his hand on his chest, gently forcing him to lie down again, wiped the blood from his lips.

'Father Fenu… Father Fenu…'he murmured, panting. 'There's something else…'

The priest brought his head lower to listen.

'I stole… in a church… I stole a diamond ring… from Nostra Signora del Miracolo… it's there… in the cartridge belt.'

The priest's brow creased in a frown, astonished and

almost offended: bandits never steal from churches.

'Why did you do this, Simone?'

'I wanted to give it to a woman, a pledge of faithfulness.'

'Well, you must hand the ring over to me and I will return it to Nostra Signora del Miracolo.'

'No; I'd like to give it... give it to Marianna... so that she can return it.'

'Very well: I will hand the ring over to Marianna so that she can return it. Is there anything else, Simone?'

'Nothing.'

So the priest crossed himself and finished pronouncing the absolution.

Then the women were admitted to the room: Marianna moved swiftly to resume her place beside Simone, but suddenly remembered the mother's presence and stood aside.

In any case she needed to set things out for administering communion to the wounded man. She took out a white tablecloth, folded it double and laid it on the table, then went to bring the lamp from the kitchen to spread a little more light. When she returned she saw the mother had brought a small candle and was holding it, lighted, between her fingers like a pale stalk from whose golden flower seeds of pearl fell all around.

The men entered as well and knelt at the end of the room, bareheaded, clutching their hats in their hands. The door remained open and the moon laid a carpet of silver before them. Outside, the nightingale was singing.

After helping the priest to lift Simone, Marianna knelt in the narrow space between the bed and the wall, with her hand firmly behind the pillow to support him and her forehead bowed to the counterpane. She heard the words of the priest as he leant over the dying man's mouth with the wafer between his fingers, and she seemed to see once again the moon standing above the mountains and the great oak in the clearing glowing like a globe. Then all was silence. She felt a hand laid on her head; Simone called her for a third time.

'Marianna!'

She looked up and saw that the priest, still wearing his stole, was staring at her intently with his luminous dark eyes.

'Marianna,' he said, 'Simone wishes to place in your hands a ring which is to be taken by you to the church of Nostra Signora del Miracolo. You'll find it in his cartridge belt. Go and see.'

She crossed the room and lifted the heavy bandolier from the bench where she had deposited it along with his coat and belt. She opened it, and inside the inner pouch she found the ring.

The metal of the ring was tarnished, almost black, but the diamond sparkled in the semi-gloom and everyone in the room saw it.

Marianna laid it on the palm of her hand and offered it to the priest; and the priest took it between two fingers and showed it to Simone.

'Is this it?'

'That's it.'

Marianna's eyes sparkled like the diamond: her heart understood everything.

'Simone,' she said holding her hand out to him, 'put the ring on my finger.'

So then his hand, which had become thin and pale, already

seared and purified by death, rose from the sheet towards the priest's. His trembling fingers took hold of the ring and slid it over Marianna's finger.

This was their wedding ceremony.

In September she went to the festival of Our Lady of the Miracle to return the ring. She and her father were guests of a wealthy property-owning family from the village of Bitti. The eldest son, who was still unmarried while all his brothers already had wives and children, found himself looking at Marianna all through the festive dinner and then while the men sang and the women listened afterwards. Seeing her pale, closed in on herself, indifferent to everything, he made inquiries to discover if she was unwell. They told him she was not, that she was like this by nature, and that she was a woman of great piety — so much so that she made an offering to Our Lady of all the jewellery she possessed. It was then that he thought to ask for her hand in marriage.

He did so only a long while afterwards, for it was necessary to consider everything carefully, before undertaking certain steps: and Marianna too requested time to make up her mind. Finally he went to find her, at the festival of the Redeemer. He was her guest, and she received him quietly and seriously; but when the moment came to give him her answer, she looked into his eyes and a trembling passed through her which seemed to shake her free from the death inside her. And she said yes, because the eyes of her suitor resembled those of Simone.

DEDALUS CELEBRATING WOMEN'S LITERATURE
2018 — 2028

Dedalus began celebrating the centenary in 2018 of women getting the vote in the UK by a programme of women's fiction. In 1918, Parliament passed an act granting the vote to women over the age of thirty who were householders, the wives of householders, occupiers of property with an annual rent of £5, and graduates of British universities. About 8.4 million women gained the vote. It was a big step forward but It was not until the Equal Franchise Act of 1928 that women over twenty-one were able to vote and women finally achieved the same voting rights as men. This act increased the number of women eligible to vote to fifteen million. Dedalus' aim is to publish six titles each year, most of which will be translations from other European languages, for the next ten years as we commemorate this important milestone.

Titles published so far are:

The Prepper Room by Karen Duve
Take Six: Six Portuguese Women Writers edited by Margaret Jull Costa
Slav Sisters: The Dedalus Book of Russian Women's Literature edited by Natasha Perova
Baltic Belles: The Dedalus Book of Estonian Women's Literature edited by Elle-Mari Talivee
The Madwoman of Serrano by Dina Salústio
Primordial Soup by Christine Leunens
Cleopatra Goes to Prison by Claudia Durastanti
The Girl from the Sea and other stories by Sophia de Mello Breyner Andresen

The Price of Dreams by Margherita Giacobino
The Medusa Child by Sylvie Germain
Days of Anger by Sylvie Germain
Venice Noir by Isabella Panfido
Chasing the Dream by Liane de Pougy
A Woman's Affair by Liane de Pougy
La Madre (The Woman and the Priest) by Grazia Deledda
Fair Trade Heroin by Rachael McGill
Co-wives, Co-widows by Adrienne Yabouza
Catalogue of a Private Life by Najwa Bin Shatwan
Baltic Belles: The Dedalus Book of Latvian Women's Literature
edited by Eva Eglaja
This was the Man (Lui) by Louise Colet
This Woman, This Man (Elle et Lui) by George Sand
The Queen of Darkness (and other stories) by Grazia Deledda
Marianna Sirca by Grazia Deledda
The Christmas Present (and other stories) by Grazia Deledda
Cry Baby by Ros Franey
The Scaler of the Peaks by Karin Erlandsson
Take Six: Six Balkan Women Writers edited by Will Firth
My Father's House by Karmele Jaio

Forthcoming titles will include:

Take Six: Six Catalan Women Writers edited by Peter Bush
Take Six: Six Latvian Women Writers edited by Jayde Will
The Dedalus Book of Knitting: Blue Yarn by Karin Erlandsson
The Victor by Karin Erlandsson
Eddo's Souls by Stella Gaitano
For more information contact Dedalus at info@dedalusbooks.com

The Queen of Darkness (and other stories)
by Grazia Deledda

The ancient traditions of Sardinia feature heavily in this early collection. The stories collected in *The Queen of Darkness*, published in 1902 shortly after Deledda's marriage and move to Rome, reflect her transformation from little-known regional writer to an increasingly fêted and successful mainstream author.

The two miniature psycho-dramas that open the collection are followed by stories of Sardinian life in the remote hills around her home town of Nuoro. The stark but beautiful countryside is a backdrop to the passions, misadventures and injustices which shape the lives of its rugged but all too human inhabitants.

£8.99   ISBN 978 1 915568 15 1   140p   B. Format

The Christmas Present (and other stories)
by Grazia Deledda

A native of Sardinia, Grazia Deledda's novels are mostly set in the rugged hills around her home town of Nuoro. Her characters reflect the difficult lives of people still constrained by ancient customs and practices. Her voice is powerful, her tone often sombre. But her wide-ranging talent had a sunnier side, revealed in many of her later works.

The Christmas Present, first published in 1930, brings together a collection of folk tales, children's stories and personal reminiscences that portray with humour and affection the lighter side of Sardinian life. This is a book that will charm and delight, opening a window on to the Sardinia of old and the formative influences on one of Italy's most important twentieth century authors.

£8.99   ISBN 978 1 915568 16 8   142p   B. Format